DEATH AND THE D'URBERVILLES

DEATH AND THE D'URBERVILLES

Tim Heald

CHIVERS
THORNDIKE

This Large Print book is published by BBC Audiobooks Ltd, Bath, England and by Thorndike Press®, Waterville, Maine, USA.

Published in 2005 in the U.K. by arrangement with Robert Hale Ltd.

Published in 2005 in the U.S. by arrangement with Jane Chelius Literary Agency.

U.K. Hardcover   ISBN 1–4056–3423–5 (Chivers Large Print)
U.K. Softcover   ISBN 1–4056–3424–3 (Camden Large Print)
U.S. Softcover   ISBN 0–7862–7804–8 (Buckinghams)

The text of this Large Print edition is unabridged.
Other aspects of the book may vary from the original edition.

Set in 16 pt. New Times Roman.

Printed in Great Britain on acid-free paper.

British Library Cataloguing in Publication Data available

Library of Congress Cataloging-in-Publication Data

Heald, Tim.
    Death and the d'Urbervilles / by Tim Heald.
       p.   cm.
    "Thorndike Press large print Buckinghams"—T.p. verso.
    ISBN 0–7862–7804–8 (lg. print : sc : alk. paper)
    1. College teachers—Fiction. 2. College teachers as authors—
    Fiction. 3. Great Britain—Fiction. 4. Hardy, Thomas, 1840–
    1928—Influence—Fiction. 5. Large type books. I. Title.
    PR6058.E167D43 2005
    823'.914—dc22   2005010824

For Little Leonel, also known as the Financial Adviser, hoping that one day he too will read Thomas Hardy and enjoy walking in Wessex.

Acknowledgements

The first four lines of *Dorset* from John Betjeman's Collected Poems © 1958 are reproduced by permission of John Murray Publishers.

CHAPTER ONE

Drip, drip, drip.

Mrs Brooks stared at the stain on the ceiling and watched it slowly enlarge. The stain was red. When she had first noticed it a minute or so earlier it had been a faint blush on the white-painted surface above her. At first it was the size of a wafer, then quite soon, the size of a man's hand. And growing. Mrs Brooks had recently had The Herons decorated from top to toe and, like any good sea-side landlady, she was grudging about the money she had to pay the painters. Now, observing the stain turn from a blush to a blemish, she felt the first stirrings of outrage.

'Those bloody D'Urbervilles,' she muttered to herself 'I knew they'd be trouble.'

She was used to unmarried couples registering under aliases and had assumed from the first that the couple who had taken the front room upstairs were an illicit item. He answered to Alec and she to Teresa or Tess which was usual enough, but the D'Urberville surname was preposterous. Most people checked in as White, Brown, Smith or Clark. She didn't care. She was guided by that arithmetical demon 'Profit and Loss'. If people chose to check in with double barrels, or three initials, or fancy foreign names with apostrophes it was all the same to her provided they paid the bills.

1

Drip, drip, drip.

Mrs Brooks was not naturally curious, but as the drops of liquid fell regularly on to her precious new carpet and created a mirror image to the desecration of her precious ceiling she could contain herself no longer. Gathering up her skirts she stepped on to a chair and thence to the table, stabbed at the liquid stain with a forefinger, withdrew it and examined it thoughtfully and with growing certainty.

It was blood.

Blood did not normally seep through the floors and ceilings of superior guest-houses in Sandbourne. Sandbourne was not that sort of place. More than a century earlier it had been described as 'This fashionable watering-place, with its eastern and its western stations, its piers, its groves of pines, its promenades, and its covered gardens'. It was still now, in 2003, genteel, civilized, the kind of south-coast English resort where Agatha Christie would have felt at home and where water was thicker than blood. Nevertheless Mrs Brooks was standing on the table of her downstairs parlour putting her finger to an ever-widening . . . well . . . bloodstain.

She had known when they arrived a few days earlier. He was a raffish, caddish creature in frayed Savile Row suiting; she soulful, tearful, full of coquettish melancholy. Mrs Brooks could smell sex and, when she saw them, she smelt it in buckets. There was something wrong too. This was not the sex between romantic runaways but

2

between a couple of unequals, the one exploited the other exploiting. It smelt incestuous, unnatural, worse than just adulterous, wrong and somehow doomed.

Mrs Brooks was seldom wrong about such matters. Seaside landladies, no matter how prim, no matter how much their houses were of well-repute, had a nose for sexual disorder and crime passionnel. And as soon as she clapped eyes on them she smelt impending doom of an almost certainly sexual nature.

But the man paid cash. In advance.

It was when the other man turned up, skeletal and jaundice-yellow, that her suspicions had been confirmed. Another absurd name, obviously false. Angel. But whether it was Angel Someone or Someone Angel she wasn't sure. He said it was his Christian name but never volunteered a surname so that Mrs Brooks was inclined to think that Angel was his only name. Avenging Angel, Angel of Mercy, Angel of Death. He had the air of leprosy and he had arrived like the Grim Reaper early in the morning at the milkman's side asking for Tess Durbeyfield but seemed almost relieved to hear that there was a woman lodging with her husband at The Herons by the name of Mrs D'Urberville. The Angel asked to see her and when Mrs Brooks went upstairs she found the woman awake and ready to see the visitor though in a state of some distress. Mrs Brooks had seen enough fallen women in her guest-house to recognize that such

3

symptoms were the norm.

There had been words, a number of them, but the landlady, listening at the keyhole had caught relatively few, despite what she would later declare in court. Suffice it to say that the words sounded mutually regretful but also recriminatory. They were angry words though bruised. Then the man called Angel left and the woman, Tess or Teresa, retreated into her quarters and gave herself over to a disconsolate moaning. Then, although we have only Mrs Brooks's words for this, she heard a man's voice, presumably Mrs D'Urberville's alleged husband. He sounded characteristically short and truculent.

Mrs Brooks was getting a bit nervous by now and, feeling guilty about her not very efficient eavesdropping, she retreated to her parlour to finish her own breakfast while her lodgers finished theirs. She was on the point of going up to take away their trays when she heard a creaking of floorboards and a rustling of garments. A few moments later she recognized the form of Mrs D'Urberville leave the room clad now in 'the walking costume of a well-to-do young lady in which she had arrived'. The only difference was that she now wore a veil over her hat and black feathers so that she could not be recognized.

At this point Mrs Brooks, somewhat perplexed, resumed her sewing, and, after a few moments, glanced up at the ceiling to see the first

4

faint blush of the stain which was to so alarm her.

Drip, drip, drip.

Otherwise silence.

Thoroughly alarmed now the landlady rushed out into the street and bumped into a passing workman whom she knew. She begged him to come into her house as she was concerned about one of her lodgers. They went upstairs to find the D'Urberville breakfast of coffee, eggs and ham completely untouched, except that the carving knife was missing.

Mrs Brooks asked the workman to go into the next-door room. This he did, only to return almost at once, ashen- or rigid-faced, with the words, 'My good God, the gentleman in bed is dead! I think he has been hurt with a knife—a lot of blood has run down upon the floor!'

Drip, drip, drip.

*   *   *

'Nice one boss,' said the girl in the tight boots, tight jeans and tight T-shirt, who had been reading the afore-mentioned words with a furrowed brow and almost scholarly expression. She cast the paper on the desk-top. 'Thomas Hardy, crime writer.'

Dr Tudor Cornwall, Reader in Criminal Studies at the University of Wessex, smiled indulgently at his most-loved, most-hated, post-graduate student and said with the

5

donnish superiority of one of the world's leading experts in his field.

'Well up to a point, Elizabeth, now let's discuss. Compare and contrast.'

CHAPTER TWO

'First off,' she said, chewing a pencil-end and looking at him almost flirtatiously in a Princess Di, under-the-eyelashes way that she knew he found disconcerting, 'the landlady's evidence is completely uncorroborated. Isn't that so?'

'I'd say so, yes,' Cornwall nodded.

'Would a court have accepted it?'

Cornwall looked thoughtful. 'In 1891 . . . difficult to say. Hardy doesn't give us a court scene. I would have thought Mrs Brooks would cut a plausible figure in the witness box but I don't know how well she would stand up under cross-examination.'

'There's no reason not to believe her,' said Elizabeth Burney. 'She's a perfectly respectable, middle-aged boarding-house-keeper and there's no motive for her to lie. On the other hand I'm not sure I entirely believe what she says.'

'Ah.' Cornwall smiled with the air of a man who has executed a particularly effective move at chess. 'Are you saying you don't believe what she says or that you don't believe the interpretation put on it?'

'We don't know precisely what interpretation was put on her evidence,' said Elizabeth. 'We don't even know whether she was called as a witness. We assume that Tess pleaded guilty in which case it would have been an open and shut case.'

'What makes you say Tess pleaded guilty?'

'She confessed to Angel Clare. She had a motive. She was there in the rooms with the husband she loathed. Her finger-prints would have been on the knife.'

Cornwall rubbed his jaw. It was sandpapery to his touch even though he had shaved with his customary efficiency. His stubble seemed to grow faster by the day now that he had turned fifty. Sometimes he wondered if he should let it go and grow a beard. It would be greyish like the hair on the top of his head, which was still comfortingly thickish, and might give him more gravitas. On the other hand he was not sure he needed more gravitas. He did not wish to be thought austere or forbidding. He liked to put his students at their ease and too many whiskers would make him look like an Old Testament prophet. Actually most of his students were already a little frightened of him though he didn't know this. What he did know was that Elizabeth Burney was extremely unfrightened of him. In fact he felt that she didn't even have the respect that a pupil should have for her

7

master. He thought she quite liked him and this was important. He did not have an all-embracing desire to be liked, the reverse if anything, but he wanted to be liked by Elizabeth. God knew why. She was maddening, difficult and young enough to be his daughter. On the other hand she was very bright and, he had reluctantly to admit, attractive. Actually this was something he tried not to admit because he knew he was almost of an age when he could be accused of being a dirty old man. And nowadays for a tutor to even think sexual thoughts about a pupil, even a postgraduate, was to court disaster. Sometimes he was afraid to give Elizabeth an alpha for an essay in case it was construed as sexual harassment.

'Sorry.' He was aware that his attention had drifted and that she was talking to him. 'Sorry,' he repeated. 'What were you saying?'

'I was saying that Hardy wasn't interested in the murder, he was interested in Tess as a woman and in the terrible things done to her by men. A Victorian novelist like Wilkie Collins was interested in crime as a puzzle. Hardy isn't. Before that I was saying that it is reasonable to assume that Tess pleaded guilty in court.'

Cornwall raised his eyebrows.

'Are you sure of that?' he asked.

'Of what?' she parried.

'First, that Hardy wasn't interested in crime

8

as a puzzle. Second, that Tess entered a guilty plea.'

It was one of the attractive features of this girl, thought Tudor to himself, that she liked intellectual or academic duels. He did too. Most of his pupils, sadly, were acquiescent to the point of being dull. It was no fun teaching young men and women who hung on your every word and committed them slavishly to paper. Little Elizabeth Burney was a real Tasmanian devil.

'It's obvious that Hardy isn't interested in crime as a puzzle,' she said, 'because when he's writing about Tess we don't even know there is a crime until the book's virtually finished. Hardy is about grief and tragedy and the inexorable nature of fate. He doesn't do twists and coincidences. He's about the President of the Immortals pulling strings. God's a puppeteer as far as Old Tom's concerned. Not even a divine clockmaker.'

'I need to think about that,' said Cornwall, recognizing that this was the verbal equivalent of asking for time-out. 'But what about Tess pleading guilty? Why wouldn't she have claimed to be innocent. Or at least mitigating circumstances. In France she'd have got off for *crime passionnel*.'

'It wasn't France, it was Wessex at the end of the nineteenth century. Very self-righteous, puritanical, male chauvinist sort of society. Still is pretty much.'

She grinned, all-gamine.

'I wouldn't have thought you'd read Hardy in Tasmania.'

'That's cheap. You know Tasmania. We have a respectable literary tradition. Trollope came calling. Peter Conrad is one of ours. Nicholas Shakespeare has come to live. You know that. A lot of our Victorian women would have been victims just like Tess. Oppressed by men and oppressed by society. We're a society founded on injustice so we empathize with Tess. That's why I have a better understanding of the book than you do. Because I'm a woman and because I'm the descendant of convicts. If she hadn't been hanged Tess would have been transported.'

She tossed her head and looked defiant, daring him to contradict her.

'Van Diemen's Land stopped being a penal colony in 1853,' he said. 'You ought to know that.'

'And you,' she said, 'know perfectly well that just because Tess was published in the 1890s doesn't mean to say that it was set in the 1890s. The countryside Hardy is describing is much more primitive than late Victorian Wessex. So I believe transportation could have been an option for Tess. She could have been an ancestor of mine. I could have been a D'Urberville.'

'Don't be ridiculous,' said Cornwall, 'and you've taken us miles off the point.'

'Which is?' She asked the question mildly but with mischief in her eyes.

'Which is to consider *Tess of the D'Urbervilles* as a crime novel and to debate my contention that while it may be a great novel it's a rotten whodunnit.'

She grinned. 'So it's all part of "what would *Macbeth* have been like if Agatha Christie had written it", or "what's the difference between Dostoevsky and Jeffrey Archer?"'

'You're deliberately trivializing,' said Cornwall. 'The point I'm making is that *Tess of the D'Urbervilles* is deeply flawed and that if Hardy had had the slightest knowledge of police procedure or forensics or even human psychology or sexuality he would have written a very different book.'

'So are you setting me an essay?'

'No,' he said, 'I'm setting myself a task, which is to rewrite *Tess* as a crime novel. I want you to go away and think about it, but I don't want it to interfere with your thesis. Merely to inform it.'

'Oh, OK.'

Elizabeth Burney's thesis was an examination of Julian Symons' famous proposition that 'The idea that detective fiction could not be written until organized detective forces existed is logically persuasive but not literally true.' It should have been a study confined almost exclusively to the nineteenth century and possibly earlier, but

11

Elizabeth's febrile imagination and subversive mentality meant that she was straying much nearer the present day. She was also completely unrestrained by the conventional wisdom that such fiction was until very recently the prerogative of the Americans, the British and to a certain extent the French. She was also disturbingly modern or even post-modern about the precise definition of 'fiction'. Postively Eagletonian though she differed from the famous Professor Terry and his ilk in possessing a prose style which was elegant and incisive. She used the English language as if it were a cross between a sabre and a scalpel. Cornwall admired her, was proud of her, and sometimes a little afraid, but he was damned if he would let any of this show.

She, for her part, was decently impressed by her tutor. Confident enough to believe, perhaps correctly, that she was brighter than he was, she acknowledged that he had almost thirty years' start on her in their chosen field. He had read more, thought more, seen more, heard more and even if she was wrong and he was actually her intellectual equal or even superior, she had to acknowledge that he knew more. So he bloody well should.

Cornwall had practically invented 'Criminal Studies'. Until he set up the department there had been departments of pathology and of forensic medicine. There had been the Police

Academy at Hendon. There had been centres of media studies and even some avant-garde departments of English where crime fiction was studied and given an arcane language comprehensible only to academics specializing in the subject. There were also departments of sociology dealing in every aspect of real-life crime but also like the Eng. Lit. people, speaking no known language only a mind-numbing form of semiotics. Cornwall was unusual in dealing in good plain English. He always said that he knew enough not to be afraid of being understood. It was only the second-rate who invented a pseudo-academic language incomprehensible to the layman. If they spoke in lay language, lay readers would know what they were talking about and recognize it for the rubbish or at best the platitudinously obvious that it actually was. And then there were the law schools. At least the lawyers spoke recognizable English. As long as there were juries to convince that was still essential. Tudor suspected that the moves to abolish the jury had nothing to do with the efficient administration of justice but rather the desire of the judiciary to retreat still further into a world in which the only people who understood them were their fellow advocates.

Cornwall's coup was to incorporate all these disparate elements into a single school. The University of Wessex's BA in Criminal Studies contained a little bit of criminal this, a little bit of criminal that and much else criminal besides. Graduates would be expected to have some knowledge of the history of the detective story and its plot and character; they would understand the basics of DNA testing and the forensic laboratory; and they would have been taught the differences between admissible and inadmissible evidence. This would not actually qualify them for being barristers or pathologists or even crime writers. Most of Cornwall's graduates went on to teach criminal studies themselves in one of the burgeoning schools imitating the movement's onelie begetter. A few became merchant bankers or investment analysts. A very few, and they often the brightest, took to crime, usually of a white collar variety. His seminars on company fraud were unusually well-attended and alarmingly creative. Only one Criminal Studies graduate had become a convicted murderer though there was no telling how many others had avoided conviction. After all, if the teaching was up to scratch, Wessex's graduate criminals would avoid being found guilty or even being found out.

This pioneering work had brought Cornwall a growing celebrity. There were books, magazine articles and, increasingly, instant opinions. These had originally been offered on matters directly pertaining to crime but now extended to such essentially non-criminal matters as the leadership of the Conservative Party, the European common currency and royal butlers. There was much talk of a major TV series though this remained as yet unmade. Tudor Cornwall was very much arriving.

His enemies, of whom there were many, were bitchily personal in the manner of the academic world, dwelling on such perceived weaknesses as his snappy little Morgan sports car and his well-concealed and therefore possibly non-existent sex life rather than the qualities of his academic achievement. Actually as academics in universities of the third or even fourth division went—and this was where Wessex found itself in most of the published league tables and in private estimations—Tudor Cornwall was pretty hot stuff. His Department of Criminal Studies was not only a pioneer, it was widely perceived to be world-class—the only world-class act in the place. No wonder his fellow academics were jealous.

As for the sports car, it was one of his few indulgences and he enjoyed driving fast with the lid down. The sex life was deliberately private and if pushed he would have to admit that it lay more in the past than the present, which did not mean that he had no hopes for the future. There was grief in the past. Tragedy even. He preferred not to think about it, but some sense that there was a ghost on his shoulder gave him an air of mild melancholy which the more vulnerable of his female students found disturbing and even attractive.

Elizabeth Burney was immune to this but not unaware. 'Cornwall looked at his watch. It said seven o'clock.

'Fancy a drink?' he asked. 'Or coffee? I feel like a glass of something and I'd appreciate the company.'

'Thanks,' she said, grinning. 'Don't mind if I do.'

She didn't really have friends either. Not yet anyway. She was a long way from home. And not long arrived.

CHAPTER THREE

It was damp outside in that peculiarly British way which made the atmosphere sodden without there actually being rain or even drizzle. The street lamps were surrounded in a halo of glistening moisture and people's breaths steamed, though it was not frosty cold, just wet and miserable and November. The streets struck Cornwall as being Dickensian though Hardyesque would have been a more appropriate word. Not that Hardy was a describer of urban landscapes being, he supposed, more of a woodlander. Cornwall often wondered if Hardy and his heroine would recognize the town. He would be surprised to find himself effigied in a seated statue but the essential structure of the place was much as it would have been just over a hundred years earlier. Discard the shop fronts and neon and this was still the small provincial market town it would have been in the nineteenth century.

Tutor and pupil walked close together, he in a belted, off-white riding mac, she in a mud-brown Driza-bone. On the corner of Jude and Bathsheba, Cornwall bought an *Evening Echo* from the wrinkled newsvendor, stuffed it in his poacher's pocket out of the damp, and then jaywalked Elizabeth across the street and in through the doors of Henchards wine bar and brasserie.

Henchards was modelled on El Vino, the Cheshire Cheese and sundry other London hostelries, some ersatz and some not. Henchards was fake through and through but in a curiously comforting way, with sawdust on the floor, cockfighting and fox-hunting pictures on the dark-brown walls and old barrels serving as haphazard partitions.

'Manage half a bottle of red?' he asked, and the girl nodded absent-mindedly as if to suggest the question was redundant though she was not a particularly heavy drinker. Nor he. But the day had been hard and the weather needed to be kept at bay. There was a large open fireplace and real logs alight, glowing and throwing out pungent smoke. Not fake at all.

'Rymill or Rockford?' he asked, naming two favourite Australian wines both of which featured unusually for the wine list of a bar/brasserie in a small Wessex town.

'We had the Rymill last time,' she said, so he ordered the Rockford and took the opened bottle and two glasses to a small table within warming distance of the fire.

'It's a neat idea,' she said, when they had removed their coats and sipped at the robust red infuriator from the Barossa.

'What?'

'Rewriting great novels in the style of pulp-fiction.'

He smiled. 'Not exactly pulp-fiction.'

'OK,' she agreed, 'we both have a vested interest in thinking crime fiction is better than pulp. Let's just say "genre". That's non-pejorative. Still a good idea.'

'Thank you. It's quite common for crime writers not to be able to understand that they're not great artists. John Creasey was in a permanent rage because critics didn't think he was as good as Dostoevsky.'

'John Creasey?' she frowned. 'Who he?'

'Founded the Crime Writers' Association. Wrote hundreds of novels but no one knows quite who really wrote them because he operated on a sort of studio basis like Titian or Rembrandt. He had a whole lot of minions

18

typing away in a big room and he'd go round looking over their shoulders and correcting what they wrote. The results went out under his own name. He had a character called "the Toff".'

'And he thought he was a great writer?'

Tudor smiled. 'So I believe,' he said.

'Make a good TV series,' she said.

'I'd thought of that. In fact my agent's set up a lunch with Larry Benjamin at Double Take to talk it through. Larry's seen an outline and he's apparently very keen.'

Cornwall took the local paper from the inside of his raincoat and shook it open. Despite having been on the inside it had lost its snap, crackle and pop and was a poor limp thing.

'Just wanted to see the latest score in Bangladesh,' he said, only half-apologetically. Like many Englishmen of his generation he was still keen on cricket, turned to the sports page first and did not think it at all rude to read a newspaper in front of a woman even when there were only two people present and he found her attractive. Tudor would have been quite hurt if someone had told him he was being boorish or old-fashioned. He regarded himself as almost painfully polite and at the very cutting edge of practically everything with the possible exception of contemporary popular music. He still thought The Who were the world's greatest band.

'Another middle order collapse,' he said to Elizabeth, who, for an Australian, was distinctly odd in that she was not the least bit interested in sport of any kind, not even when the males were good-looking and wore tight shorts.

'Hey!' she exclaimed, almost choking on her Rockford shiraz. 'Do you believe in coincidences, or do you believe in coincidences?'

Tudor was shaking his head, irritated but unsurprised. 'Just when you think they've sorted themselves out they go and get themselves out to a string of long-hops and half volleys,' he said, mysteriously.

'Listen!' she said loudly. 'BODY IN B AND B, BLED TO DEATH IN BED. MISSING WOMAN SOUGHT. "BLOOD CAME RIGHT THROUGH CEILING" SAYS LANDLADY.'

'Hey, I was reading that!' he said crossly. Elizabeth had snatched the newspaper from him and was reading out loud. First she repeated the screaming headlines, glaring at him with a sort of manic triumph.

Tudor shook his head.

'You could call it coincidence,' he said, 'but you'd be stretching a point. That sort of thing happens all the time, especially at the seaside. People who hardly know each other come for a dirty weekend. Things go wrong. They have too much to drink. There's a row which starts over something trivial but then turns into a serious shouting match and one of them stabs the other with a sharp instrument, or hits them with a blunt one, and suddenly before you know where you are you've got a newspaper headline saying "BODY IN B AND B".'

'Well excuse me.' Elizabeth sounded truculent. 'If you don't think it's a weird coincidence, then listen to this . . .' And she read on, *'The body of a man was found stabbed to death in a bedroom of the Mon Repos Guest-house in Gallipoli Street, Sandbourne, yesterday.*

'Said landlady, Mrs Rose Anderson, 48, "This is a very distressing incident for all of us at Mon Repos. I first became aware that something was wrong when I saw a red patch on the ceiling of my own lounge which is on the ground floor immediately below the bedroom occupied by the deceased and his wife or partner."'

'Do you really think she said that?' asked Tudor. 'No one talks like that in real life. Only in local newspapers.'

'So local newspaper reporters have tin ears,' she said, 'so what's odd about that? You don't win Pulitzers on the Wessex *Evening Echo.* You can bet your bottom dollar though that the landlady's name is Rose Anderson and that she's forty-eight and she saw blood on the ceiling and she's distressed. As is everyone at Mon Repos.'

'Particularly if you'd just had the place redecorated.'

She glanced at him sharply and

21

reproachfully.

'You're muddling your rewrite of Thomas Hardy with what actually happened in Sandbourne as reported here in the *Echo*. You're confusing fact and fiction.'

'Fact and fiction *is* confusing,' said Cornwall. 'That's what makes a great novelist great. You believe what he tells you even more than what the media tell you. You believe the printed page more than what you see in the street.'

She sighed. 'That's a real academic's argument. Argument for the sake of argument. Ivory-tower stuff. Anyway listen to the next paragraph and tell me if you still think there isn't something odd going on.'

He started to interrupt but thought better of it, took another mouthful of the blood-red wine and settled back in his chair to listen.

'*The deceased,*' she read, '*was described by police as being a caucasian male in his late thirties to early forties. He had registered at the hotel as Mr Alex or Alec Durberville. His wife or partner was booked in as Theresa or Tessa Durberville. Mrs Durberville, believed to be in her early to mid-thirties, of medium build with brown hair and a slightly sallow complexion is being sought by Sandbourne police who are anxious to question her with regard to her husband's death. It is not known whether foul play is suspected.*'

She put the paper down and fixed him with

a stare which said 'game, set and match.'

He looked back, poker-faced, then swallowed hard and conceded.

'That *is* a little bit surprising,' he said, looking suitably surprised. 'Would you mind reading it again?'

She picked up the paper and reread the offending paragraph. When she had finished, she laid the paper down again and they both took a glug of wine but said nothing.

After a while Elizabeth said, 'Not exactly a usual name, is it? Particularly when you take the Christian names into account.'

'Well.' You could almost see the cogs whirring in Cornwall's brain. 'It's too much of a coincidence to be a coincidence.'

'Huh?' she ventured, eyebrows arched.

'As you say,' he began slowly, 'D'Urberville or Durbeyfield which is the Anglo-Saxon version isn't exactly a usual name though it has a genuine factual basis. Hardy took it from some gravestones or stained-glass windows at Bere Regis not far from where he lived. It's conceivable that this man D'Urberville really was a D'Urberville, a descendant of some Norman aristocrat who came over with William for the Conquest in 1066. However, as you rightly say, it's unlikely that he would have the same Christian name as the character in the Thomas Hardy book and inconceivable that his wife or partner should, really, in real life be called after Tess of the D'Urbervilles.'

'Even I'd got that far,' she said, a shade petulantly, 'But where do you go from there?'

'Not very far without examining some evidence. Birth certificate would be a start. Passport. I'd be amazed if either of them said D'Urberville. Let alone Alec.'

'So it's an assumed name. An alias.'

'If not, then,' said Tudor, 'the Pope's a . . . well never mind, you know what I mean. Yes. He, whoever he was, made it up.'

'But why?' She frowned.

'Too early to tell.'

'And dying in a boarding-house in Sandbourne with blood staining the ceiling of the room downstairs. Are you saying that's just coincidence?'

Cornwall didn't answer for a while. Then he said, thoughtfully, 'You can't deny coincidence. It's a fact of life though I'm sceptical about the concept of *mere* coincidence.'

'Meaning?'

'Meaning,' he said, 'that coincidence usually contains elements which make it predictable rather than random or haphazard. You know, you bump into someone at the far ends of the earth when you least expect to see them but when you come to examine the reasons for your both being there you realize that the apparent coincidence is far from merely coincidental.'

'So you're saying that the fact that a man called Alec D'Urberville dies in a Sandbourne bed and breakfast in identical circumstances to the death of a man with the same name in a Victorian novel is coincidental but not merely so.'

'Nicely put,' said Cornwall in donnish mode.

'But what about the fact that you were in the process of rewriting the same novel and had just read me the very scene in which the landlady sees the blood staining the ceiling of her sitting-room. And discovers the body.'

'Ah,' said Cornwall, even more donnishly, 'if we're being accurate, and I mean accurate and not pedantic, in the book the landlady goes out into the street and it's a passer-by who finds the corpse. In this latest incident the landlady appears to have found Alec herself'

'Can't have everything,' she said.

'Quite,' he agreed. 'And as for the death taking place just as I was rewriting the same scene, well . . .'

Another long pause during which they both drank deep and gave every impression of thought.

Eventually Cornwall spoke.

'You know how difficult it is to prove plagiarism.'

'Not really,' she said. 'If you copy something out word for word it's pretty bloody obvious.'

'Well maybe,' he mused. 'I'm not even sure of that, but there's a form of alleged plagiarism which is a greyer area. It's why there's no copyright in ideas or in titles. Who

25

invented the steam engine, for instance—
Trevithick or Stephenson? Or the wheel? Or
dynamite? Or almost anything. It's a historical
fact, is it not, that people in completely
different parts of the world can have the same
idea at the same time.'

She stared at him, not understanding.

'What exactly are you saying?' she asked
eventually, for he did not appear to be about
to explain.

'It's only a working hypothesis,' he said, 'but
I'm suggesting that the man found dead as
reported in the *Echo* may have had much the
same idea as me. Hundreds of thousands of
people have read *Tess of the D'Urbervilles.* Why
should I be the only person who wanted to
rewrite it?!'

CHAPTER FOUR

Cornwall decided to use his reworking of
Hardy's *Tess* as the core of his seminar for
third-year students on 'Meaning, Motive and
Murder in the Nineteenth Century Novel:
1841-1891'. The title had the sort of resonance
appreciated by academics and, more
importantly by those who inspected and
assessed academics and the universities of
which they were part. The use of 'Meaning'
was deliberate and a private joke of Cornwall's

who was bright and old-fashioned enough to know that the common denominator in most new university courses was their lack of meaning. Ambiguity and obfuscation were essential in the establishment of new subjects for degrees and diplomas. If you understood what the teachers were talking about it was, virtually by definition, no bloody good.

The dates 1841 and 1891 not only represented an exact half-century, they were also the publication dates of Edgar Allan Poe's *Murders in the Rue Morgue* and, of course, of *Tess.* Not many assessors or inspectors knew this and Cornwall enjoyed exposing their ignorance, though to do so was to risk bad marks which in turn could lead to a reduction in his department's funding or even a loss of tenure itself. Part of the course was 'Edgar Allan Poe and Thomas Hardy: compare and contrast' but to have put it like that would have invited immediate derision.

'As soon as we've described the discovery of the corpse,' he said, 'we change gear. Think of the classic obituary.' He paused a touch theatrically and looked round the little class with a questioning air. 'Well,' he continued, 'think of the classic obituary. Go on. And when you've thought of it, tell me how it changes gear.'

There was an uncomfortable shuffly silence with much looking at the ground and avoiding his eyes. Eventually, he said, 'OK, Freddie.

Give me a classic obituary opening.'

Freddie was a shambling blond Old Etonian with an oafish expression and a languid drawl which disguised a perfectly adequate intelligence. Better than adequate actually. He would easily manage the requisite good second-class degree and could aspire to a first if he exerted himself if it weren't for the fact that the university tried very hard to avoid giving first-class degrees to students who came to them from the private sector. Even admitting them was to court governmental and official disapproval but to give them top-class degrees would have been perceived as appallingly elitist and would have attracted swingeing fines and punishments .

'OK, yuh,' said Freddie. 'Well, how about *"Doctor Tudor Cornwall who died yesterday was one of Britain's leading criminalists. As head of the ground-breaking Department of Criminal Studies at the University of Wessex he was at the cutting edge of the academic study of crime and the criminal. He was also a prolific author and broadcaster who probably made more money and acquired a greater reputation than the most nefarious British criminal."* '

There was a Mexican wave of a titter and Freddie looked rather pleased with himself. Tudor generously—and genuinely—joined in the laughter.

'That's very good, Freddie. If I didn't know, I'd say you'd been practising. Did you mean to

28

say *criminalist?*

'I think so sir, yes.'

'For Christ's sake don't call me *sir*,' said Tudor. 'I should have thought you'd have learned that by now.'

'Sorry, sir,' said Freddie flushing. 'I mean, sorry.'

'So I should hope,' Tudor was cross with himself. He shouldn't have barked. 'I'm sorry,' he said, 'but you know how I hate it.'

He did too. His school hadn't been as grand as Freddie's but it was still the sort of place where you called masters and even prefects 'sir'. Cornwall could just about manage marginal deference but only with people who earned it. He hated calling people 'sir' when he despised them, or even when he regarded himself as their equal.

'I don't think you'll find criminalist in the dictionary,' he said. 'What's wrong with criminologist?'

'I thought it was a bit old-fashioned and narrow,' said Freddie. 'Criminologists are really only interested in real-life crime and criminals and only from a narrow perspective. What we do is, well, you know, more all-embracing, less exclusive.'

'I'm glad you think so,' said Cornwall. 'Crime is all-embracing and not in the least bit exclusive. It's part of what makes it so fascinating. So, OK, you've done your first paragraph of obit with the obligatory "who

29

died yesterday" plus a snappy paragraph explaining why I'm worth memorializing. Now what?'

He looked round the room, amused as always, at the way they all avoided eye-contact and gazed at the floor or ceiling. They were like so many ostriches. Did they assume he couldn't see them being evasive? He supposed so. It was an odd quirk of group psychology. He wondered if it had a criminal application or connotation. Most things did.

'Tamsin,' he said, addressing a pretty Cornish girl at the back of the class who was pretending to be absorbed in note-taking but was actually just doodling, 'give us the obituary gear-change. What comes after the stand-first?'

Tamsin looked up, with a startled *what-me?* expression. She had piercing blue eyes, very white skin, very black hair.

'Umm' she said. 'Well, you have the news of the death and then the headline summary and then you clear your throat and slip into straightforward narrative, starting at the beginning. So you'd write *"Tudor Stuart Somerset Cornwall was born on* er, I'm guessing but let's say *13 April 1950 and educated at."*'

Everyone laughed at Tamsin's inventive second and third Christian names and Tudor said, 'You all seem remarkably witty today.' He said it slightly patronizingly but with enough of a grin to take the edge off a remark which

30

could otherwise have seemed hostile. 'But good, Tamsin, that's right, that's exactly what the obituary does. You do the death, the reason for thinking the deceased significant, and then it's more or less straightforward narrative with a final paragraph about wife, husband, next of kin and perhaps a reference to the long fatal illness bravely born.'

Now they really *were* all taking notes. Note-taking was a habit he privately disparaged. It smacked too much of teaching by rote, of studying by numbers and yet it was part of the system. He knew that but he craved the unorthodox and unconventional. Note-taking was about sticking to rules. Crime was about breaking them. Nevertheless . . .

'The classic obituary follows a particular form,' he said. 'It's like a sonnet or a game of chess. The ingredients are infinitely variable but the framework is precise and well established. The classic crime novel is similar. You begin as I have done with my version of *Tess* and as Thomas Hardy did not with his version, with the murder itself. Then, just as in the obituary, you clear your throat, change gear and begin the narrative.'

'But Dr Cornwall . . .'

A young man in a denim jacket with dark designer stubble, spiky hair and bags under his eyes wanted to make a point. His name was Karl. He was a vegan and a passionate pacifist.

'Do call me Tudor.' Even as he said it he

wondered why he made such a meal out of mode of address. What did it matter? You could be on intimate terms with someone you called sir or ma'am, couldn't you? Like the Prince of Wales and his Mum. And conversely you could be distant and unknowable while calling someone by their Christian name, or by such terms of endearment as *darling*, or, *my lover*. Indeed you couldn't have betrayal without it being preceded by intimacy. Or could you? These were the sorts of question you asked each other in Criminal Studies. The confidence trickster was at the heart of crime. Theft, fraud, rape and murder were more often than not perpetrated by those whom the victims trusted. It was friends you had to be suspicious of not enemies. That, God help him, was part of what Tudor Cornwall taught.

'Carry on, Karl,' he said, snapping out of his thirty-second day-dream.

'Detective,' said Karl, in his unattractive nasal Mockney accent, 'in a crime novel there's a detective. We get to meet him in chapter two. Maybe earlier. But Hardy has no detective.'

'Good point,' Cornwall agreed. It was important to encourage students even when the points they raised were as obvious as Karl's. Perhaps it was even more important when the points were easy and obvious. Karl needed encouraging.

'In Hardy's *Tess*,' Cornwall continued, 'we

begin with Tess's tipsy father coming home from the pub and then we meet Tess. Good scene actually. All the village girls in virgin white dresses and these three upper-class brothers come hiking across the countryside and the youngest joins in the girls' dance. And he notices Tess and Tess notices him and the reader knows immediately that this is love at first sight but on the printed page the opportunity is lost, the moment missed. Would that have happened if Hardy were a crime writer?'

'It might if he were a really good crime writer.' This was from Frances. She was from Newcastle-on-Tyne, a northern lass with a strong Geordie accent, working class and chippily proud of the fact. She was passionate about Newcastle United Football Club and Newcastle Brown Ale. After a few pints of the stuff she sang a passably tuneful version of United's war song, 'The Bladon Races'.

'A really good crime writer might start with a scene like that. It's only the second-raters who do the obvious.'

Cornwall smiled, 'There is a school of thought that says that even the term "crime-writing" is pejorative,' he said. 'Agatha Christie, whom it is fashionable to deride, is a crime writer but someone like John le Carré is said to *transcend the genre*. But at the end of the day le Carré is a crime writer—or thriller writer—and that's another distinction we'll consider at another time. The people who say that writers like le Carré *transcend the genre* are missing the point, surely, which is that writers like le Carré are fantastically good. They don't *transcend the genre*: they may move it forward, take it into areas that it hasn't previously reached, but they are still writing a particular kind of story which fits into the category which we, here in Criminal Studies at the University of Wessex, choose to call crime writing. Do we agree?'

He was aware that he was on the verge of sounding pompous. Bad move.

'Are you saying that a good crime novelist is better than a bad literary novelist?' This was from Freddie. It was a question expecting an affirmative response.

'What do you think, Freddie?' he asked.

'I think le Carré's better than Martin Amis,' said Freddie, 'so, yuh. I guess I think a good crime writer is better than a bad literary writer.'

'Are you saying that Martin Amis is a bad writer?' asked Tamsin, bridling with Celtic indignation, 'I think Martin Amis is like great.'

'But we're not disputing that Amis and le Carré write in different categories?'

'Martin's dad wrote crime fiction,' said Freddie. 'He wasn't much good at it. Give me Ian Fleming any day.'

Cornwall smiled. He enjoyed discursiveness, hated lessons which stuck to the text book.

Even so.

'Aren't we getting a little off the point?' he asked.

Nobody said anything, but despite the silence there was a clear collective group affirmative. They knew they were off the point.

'Remind us Karl of the point off which are wandering.'

Karl looked spikily rebellious. There was no particular reason for this. It was just his preferred stance. He thought it was smart.

'The detective,' he said. 'You were asking what Hardy would have done after the landlady sees the blood on her ceiling and the body's discovered. I said he'd have introduced his detective. But the most important reason that Hardy isn't a crime writer is that he *didn't* have a detective.'

'Possibly,' said Tudor, 'so let us now consider the detective.'

CHAPTER FIVE

Eddie Trythall was Cornwall's favourite detective. The two men had known each other for more years than either cared to remember and their relationship was a curious half-open secret. The Wessex Constabulary would have been officially compelled to ban their meetings if they had officially known about them but as, unofficially, the Constabulary rather approved of the link between them and academia they turned a blind eye. Tudor connived in this and it suited him too. His reputation and livelihood depended on sources such as DCS Trythall but the more shadowy they were the better. An aura of cloak and dagger enhanced his position. He was supposed to be a man of mystery in more ways than one.

In earlier days, when Tudor was a common or garden lecturer and Eddie a mere Detective Constable, they used to meet on the squash court and adjourn for a couple of ruminative pints afterwards. Now that their squash-playing days were behind them and the one was a famous head of department and media pundit while the other was a Detective Chief Superintendent running the whole of Wessex CID they still met outside the office and on neutral ground.

Once a month they lunched at Sandbourne's Imperial Hotel, a dead-duke-upstairs establishment, all antimacassar and blue-rinse, miniature poodles, yellow cardigans and crêpes suzettes. The place reeked of faded anonymity and 'gin and it'. Trythall and Cornwall met for tea or coffee in the Garden Lounge if they needed to talk outside their monthly lunches. God knew who the people who frequented the Imperial were. There were precious few of them and 'frequented' was the wrong word. People who went to the Imperial 'solitaried'. They never came back. Trythall and Cornwall were the Imperial's only regulars—more regular even than the staff who seldom spoke any known language or had a more than rudimentary idea of how to serve food or drink. The staff turnover was enormous. Cornwall reckoned the Imperial was a holding camp or clearing station for illegal immigrants. You came in from Albania or wherever in a hidden compartment at the bottom of a heavy goods vehicle and did a couple of weeks at the Imperial, Sandbourne, before being assigned to a more permanent abode up north.

The tea that afternoon was the usual dark stewed stuff and came in a heavy EPNS pot. Cornwall arrived first and ordered it from a lugubrious youth with lank black hair and a downy moustache. After some deliberation he also asked for a couple of slices of fruit cake which proved as dry and ancient as he expected. It was ever thus and he drew some satisfaction from it. There was something to be said for constants in this uncertain world.

Trythall smelt of Balkan Sobranie when he turned up five minutes later puffing slightly. He had put on weight recently, unlike his old squash opponent who was annoyingly thin.

'Sorry,' said Trythal. 'Traffic's a bugger.' He gazed round the room and shook his head.

'Beats me how this place keeps open,' he said.

Trythall always said this when he came into the Imperial. It was as much part of the ritual as the stewed tea and the stale fruit cake.

'It's a front,' said Tudor. 'Must be.'

This was what he always said too.

'What for?'

'How should I know?' said Tudor. 'You're the detective and it's your patch, not mine.'

These exchanges were like the opening sentences of matins or the mass. They had to be got through before real conversation could begin. 'Hear what comfortable words . . .' They were like the beginning of the Ceremony of the Keys at the Tower of London, hallowed by years of repetition.

'Halt, who goes there?'

'The keys.'

'Whose keys?'

'Her Majesty Queen Elizabeth the Second's keys.'

Neither man would have been happy to begin with original or spontaneous words for they were both, in their different ways, creatures of habit.

'I suppose you want to know about the D'Urberville case?' said Trythall. He was looking more than usually gingery today, thought Cornwall. The freckles seemed more orange as he got older and there were tufts of red hair sticking out of his ears. His tweed jacket bulged and bagged at the pockets and the corduroy trousers did the same at the knees. They were held up by braces. He looked like old man Durbeyfield in the Hardy novel coming home tipsy from the Pure Drop Inn. Completely unthreatening. It was one of several things which made him such a good cop.

'How did you know I wanted to be told about the D'Urberville case?'

'Give me a break.' The policeman grinned. 'Just because I look stupid doesn't mean I am stupid. You should know that by now.'

'Oh, OK.' Tudor grinned back.

They both drank tea and winced.

'First of all his name wasn't D'Urberville,' said Trythall.

'You could have fooled me.'

'I doubt that.' The idea seemed to amuse the chief superintendent, examining his slice of fruit cake as if it were the prime suspect in a murder investigation. He fingered a large currant and looked as if he were on the verge of declaring it the guilty party. Instead he said, 'There was a passport among his effects with the name Albert Smith in it. On slightly closer examination we found he'd used a number of names over the years; D'Urberville was much the most exotic. He seems to have preferred it to most of the others. Once or twice he seems to have given himself a title: Sir Alec D'Urberville. Affected an Old Etonian bow tie when he was laying claim to the baronetcy.'

'That's almost as much of a give-away as

Old Etonian braces,' said Cornwall. 'I take it he had form.'

'Spent almost as much of his life at Her Majesty's pleasure as he did at his own, though pleasure's not the word I'd use.'

'What were the convictions for?'

'Oh,' Eddie Trythall sighed, 'much as you'd expect. Credit-card fraud, swindling old ladies out of their savings, betting scams, falsifying second-hand car mileages, breaking and entering, petty theft. Petty everything really. He wasn't much good at any of it but you can't help admiring his chutzpah. He even tried to pass himself off as a retired squadron-leader in a golf club. Complete with a DFC. Claimed to be a Falkland veteran, Gulf War, Bosnia. He was a vicar once, but Sir Alec D'Urberville Bt., gentleman of leisure, private means and no very fixed abode was his preferred persona.'

'But who was he really?'

'God knows,' said Trythall. 'I don't think *he* did. Became the victim of his own fantasies, duped by his own confidence trickery.'

'I know,' said Cornwall, 'he felt he was a baronet, therefore he *was* a baronet; he thought he was educated at Eton therefore he *was* at Eton.'

'That's right,' Trythall extricated another currant from the cake and eyed it suspiciously. 'Some of us are who we think we are even though all the evidence suggests something quite different. Smith/D'Urberville was one of those.'

Cornwall poured them both more tea even though it was stewed and cooling fast.

'So what happened?' he asked.

'You read the papers,' said Trythall.

'Yes,' said Cornwall, 'but what happened?'

'He died. Stabbed. Bled to death.'

'By whom?'

'Person or persons unknown.' Trythall smiled wolfishly. '*Cherchez la femme. Crime passionnel.* Why is it that the French have all the words for this sort of stuff?'

Cornwall shrugged. 'There are perfectly good words in the English language. They just don't have quite the same *je ne sais quoi.* The woman you're seeking is presumably Mrs or should I say "lady" D'Urberville?'

'Who else?'

'You think she killed him?'

Eddie looked Cornwall in the eyes as if to stare him down in the ocular equivalent of arm-wrestling.

'You know as well as I do that there's no such thing as an open-and-shut case, but on the face of it this comes as near as one's ever likely to. Couple check into boarding-house; landlady hears raised voices; female party does bunk; bloodstains appear on ceiling; body in bed with domestic knife sticking out of it. QED if you'll pardon my French again.'

'Fingerprints?'

'His will be on it and so will hers. But we

can't prove that until we've found her.'

'Where are you looking?'

'Everywhere. The description's not great. Could be anyone. On the other hand I doubt she'll have much in the way of resources. She'll run out of cash before long. Give herself up most probably.'

'Tried Stonehenge?'

'No. Why?'

'Haven't you read the book?' Tudor assumed, on the whole, that everyone was conversant with *Tess of the D'Urbervilles*. Perhaps it wouldn't have been on every senior policeman's core curriculum, but while Trythall might not be in the same league as an egg-head like Adam Dalgliesh, the P. D. James detective who actually wrote poetry, he was nobody's fool and had a perfectly decent degree from a perfectly decent university.

'I could never be doing with Hardy,' said Trythall. 'Too gloomy for my taste. It always seemed to be pouring with rain and everyone's doomed and miserable.'

'Just like real life,' said Cornwall teasingly.

'Maybe that's why I don't care for him. I get enough of real life in real life. Now you mention it there was an old copy of the book at the bedside. School prize. He won it for some English essay when he was fourteen or fifteen.'

'Not stupid?'

'No,' said Trythall. 'Miserable and doomed

42

maybe but not stupid. So why Stonehenge?'

Tudor rubbed his jaw thoughtfully and felt the rasping of stubble. It was like running his thumb along the side of a Swan Vesta matchbox. Sandpaper. Time was when he'd been a smooth man. Now in middle-age he was belatedly becoming a designer stubble sort of bloke.

'This is probably silly,' he said, 'but in the book the Tess character stabs the D'Urberville character to death, then flits off with her first husband, and ends up sleeping on a sacrificial slab at Stonehenge. All very symbolic.'

'All very Thomas Hardy if you ask me.'

The presumed asylum-seeking waiter stomped over to them and asked if they'd like more tea. They declined and sat moodily staring at the EPNS pot which the waiter pointedly did not clear away.

Tudor broke the silence.

I've always thought,' he said, 'that Tess would have worked better as a classic crime novel than the slightly over-the-top Victorian melodrama that Hardy actually created. Now suddenly, just as I'm attempting to prove it up in my ivory tower someone down here in the real world seems to have had the same idea.'

Eddie Trythall felt in his pocket, pulled out his pipe, stuck it in his mouth and started to go through the messy and frankly anti-social business of stuffing it with tobacco and setting fire to it. He had just managed, after much sucking and gurgling, to produce a blue smoke-cloud, when the lank-haired waiter came hurrying over to advise him that the Garden Lounge was a no-smoking area.

The detective chief superintendent cursed colourfully and set the smouldering pipe down on the tea tray.

'So you're telling me that the D'Urberville woman or whoever she is, is going to stagger up to Stonehenge and take a kip on a sacrificial stone.'

'I think its worth a look,' said Tudor.

'She'd never get in,' said Trythall. 'It's an English Heritage site. The public aren't allowed within a hundred yards of the stones. They've got 24-hour security cameras, sniffer dogs, barbed wire, thugs in uniform.'

'Not what it was in the 1890s,' conceded Tudor. 'But I still think it's worth a look.'

He summoned the waiter and paid the bill.

'You'll keep in touch won't you?' said Tudor, as they side-stepped an elderly blue-rinse with a zimmer and almost cannoned into her be-toupeed escort.

'If you like,' said Eddie, 'though I don't think it's as interesting as you're trying to make out. Poor old stiff just nicked an exotic name out of an old prize book and used it as his working moniker. Apart from that, like I say, it's open and shut. A classic domestic.'

'You could say the same about the novel,' said Tudor, smiling, as they emerged into the

44

damp dark outside the Imperial's mahogany revolving doors. A top-hatted porter bulging out of a frock coat asked if he could get a taxi and seemed irritated when they both said no.

'Say what?' asked Trythall.

'That *Tess of the D'Urbervilles* was a classic open-and-shut domestic. That's not what professors of English literature call it but . . . well, let's see.'

They wished each other good night and headed off back into their respective worlds, each convinced that it was theirs that contained the greater truth, but united in the belief that if you wanted a real flight from reality you had only to seek refuge in the Imperial Hotel.

CHAPTER SIX

Tranter Reuben threw down The Times *in exasperation.*

'It is a capital mistake, Ledlow,' he said, 'to theorize before one has data. Now here The Thunderer *has a theory informed entirely by prejudice. I have always heard it said that Delane thought first and uttered later. Not the new man whoever he may be. Thunder, thunder, thunder . . . all noise and no substance. So the Australian banks in Melbourne and Sydney are collapsing and the workers in the Antipodes are*

revolting and lo, The Times *constructs a theory, The editor who writes for himself has a fool for a contributor. It has long been an axiom of mine that little things are infinitely the most important. Yet* The Thunderer *sees only the big things, and, seeing only the big things, is struck by its own lightning.'*

Reuben rubbed mist from the window and peered out at the passing countryside.

'Will you take a whisky and ginger wine, sir? There is a decided nip in the air.'

'You have the wherewithal, Ledlow? You are a capital fellow. What a gentleman would do without a gentleman's gentleman a gentleman will never know.'

Tranter Reuben rubbed his hands together and blew on them. He and Ledlow were the only two occupants of this particular compartment on the 4.37 London to Wintoncester Express. Reuben was dressed in the tweedy, wintry garb of an English gentleman; Ledlow in the more sombre garments of an English manservant. Both were hatted and mufflered for the train was almost as cold within as the countryside without.

'It seems strange,' ventured Ledlow as he mixed the warming libation, 'to be leaving the Great Wen for tranquil Wessex and yet to be journeying from peace and harmony to bloody murder,'

'Ah, Ledlow, Ledlow,' said Reuben, accepting a glass of whisky and ginger with a grateful smile, 'you forget that I am myself a man of Wessex,

46

born and bred. It is my belief, founded upon my experience, that the lowest and vilest alleys of London do not present a more dreadful record of sin than does the smiling and beautiful countryside.'

'Is that so, sir?' Ledlow had a glass of his mixture as well and sipped it sitting opposite his master as if he were his equal which, to an outside observer he might very well have been, were it not for the subtle differences in dress, demeanour and speech. Perhaps only an Englishman could have recognized the subtle distinctions between servant and master for they were so understated that to a foreigner they would have seemed quite invisible.

Tranter Reuben was that curious phenomenon virtually extinguished by the holocaust of the world wars of the twentieth century, the man of independent means. Reuben had no visible means of support yet he lived a life of enviable bachelor comfort in Albany chambers, ministered to by the trusty Ledlow, dining off lobster and partridge, drinking fine claret and hock, belonging to several clubs in St James's, taking the waters at Karlsbad, strolling along the front at Cannes, striding through Alps and Pyrenees, attending the opera in Milan and Vienna and generally leading the life of a civilized person of leisure.

In so far as he actually did *anything it was to be a member of that elite fraternity, the band of the great detectives: men such as Hercule Poirot,*

Lord Peter Wimsey, Albert Campion, Roderick Alleyne, Nigel Strangeways and the legendary Sherlock Holmes himself. Like them, Tranter was independent, literate and the very devil when it came to solving puzzles. He was not a policeman. Indeed he had a genial contempt for the average plod while they naturally regarded him with awe and admiration. As, of course, did Ledlow.

'Do you believe, sir,' asked Ledlow, 'that she dunnit?'

'That is what we are here to establish, Ledlow. I have my doubts as any true detective must until he has established the facts. She has confessed to the crime. That is a fact and a deuced awkward one. Nevertheless it is not an insurmountable obstacle to the task of proving the wretched woman's innocence. If, as I am disposed to believe, the balance of her mind is disturbed then this so-called confession may be swiftly dismissed.'

'Try telling that to the jury,' said Ledlow, squinting out at the gathering gloom of late autumnal Wessex.

No date had yet been fixed for the D'Urberville trial which would be in the city's Great Hall where Sir Walter Raleigh had once been sentenced to be beheaded and where King Arthur's Round Table hung upon a wall. More than half a century later it was the scene of the trial of Lord Montagu of Beaulieu, charged with homosexual offences, in one of the most notorious cases of the twentieth century and one which was to change the law belatedly and dramatically. It was a trial chamber steeped in history.

Reuben's role in the matter was, as always, unofficial. That of the great detective nearly always was. In this particular case he was a friend of Emmeline Pankhurst, the pioneer feminist. Mrs Pankhurst had been appalled by the D'Urberville case as reported, in terms distinctly unflattering to Tess, in the national Press. Knowing that newspapers were, like practically everything in Victorian England, an exclusively male preserve, she had read between the lines and concluded that Tess was one of life's victims and moreover, that creature dear to her heart, a female victim and a victim victimized on account of her sex. Tess was where she was because she was a woman. That was enough to take Emmeline Pankhurst to Wintoncester Gaol, to gain admission, to be allowed to speak with the disconsolate Tess and to persuade her at least marginally to take an interest in her well-being and her fate. She had not persuaded Tess to change her plea but she had persuaded her to accept her friendship. That friendship extended to the point of persuading Tranter Reuben to investigate the murder and to be allowed to interview the unfortunate woman who confessed to having perpetrated it.

It was to that interview that Reuben and the faithful Ledlow were now proceeding.

49

'Not sure about the names.'

'Why not?'

Elizabeth Burney looked thoughtful. Eventually she said, 'Do I have to have a reason?'

'Not if you're just being the average reader, no,' said Tudor, 'but if you're studying for a PhD in Criminal Studies then emphatically, yes. Sorry but I'm looking for intellectual rigour here, not just gut reaction.'

'I suppose I can just about cope with Ledlow,' she said, 'but Tranter Reuben is too obviously contrived. I mean who could possibly imagine someone called *Tranter Reuben*? It's a name that you just know has been invented by a cutesy-poo novelist.'

'I thought you read Hardy in Tasmania?'

'We did.'

'Well then, what about "Friends Beyond"? It's possibly the most famous poem he ever wrote:

William Dewey, Tranter Reuben, Farmer
     Ledlow late at plough,
  Robert's kin and John's and Ned's.
And the Squire, and Lady Susan, lie in
     Mellstock Churchyard now!'

Parodied, of course, by Betjeman who wrote:

Rime Intrinsica, Fontmell Magna, Sturminster
                    Newton and Melbury Bubb,
Whist upon whist upon whist drive in Institute,
                    Legion and Social Club.
Horny hands that hold the aces which this
                    morning held the plough
While Tranter Reuben, T.S. Eliot, H.G. Wells
                    and Edith Sitwell lie in Mellstock
                    Churchyard now.

'Note how Tranter Reuben is the only person to appear in the original and the parody. He is one of the great unexplored characters in English literature. He is crying out for reinvention and discovery.'

'We didn't do Hardy's poems only the novels,' said the girl sulkily. 'And I was always taught that Betjeman only wrote doggerel. In any case you're just showing off. It's obvious.'

'Not at all.' Tudor was affronted. 'I don't show off. It's not in my nature.'

This was not true but the girl let it pass.

'All that great detective stuff is silly,' she said. 'No proper writer would invent a character like that. And certainly not in 1891.'

Tudor sighed. 'As Reuben himself said, "it is a capital mistake to theorize before you have data". You simply don't have the date. In other words, you don't know what you're talking

51

about. What book was first published in 1891?'

'*Tess of the D'Urbervilles,*' she said, with an 'as every school-boy knows' expression of truculence.

Cornwall smiled his characteristically wintry smile which his enemies found arrogant and insufferable.

'*What other* book?' he asked wearily.

'I don't know,' she said. 'What *other* book?'

'The *Adventures of Sherlock Holmes,*' he said, with ill-concealed triumph, 'by Sir Arthur Conan Doyle. So you see, dear girl, just as Thomas Hardy was creating poor, tragic, traumatized Tess, so Conan Doyle was creating the first of the great detectives. Tess and Sherlock are exact contemporaries.'

The pause was even longer than usual this time. She knew that she had come off worse but she was damned if she would admit it and she was cross. It didn't take much to make her angry and the easiest way to fire her up was to be a patronizing Pom and when it came to patronizing Poms there were few, in her estimation, who were as Pommy and as patronizing, as Doctor Tudor bloody Cornwall.

'Well, I don't care. I don't like your character, Tranter Reuben. I don't believe in him. I think it's a silly name even if Hardy used it in a poem and I don't like the way he talks. I don't believe in that either. All that pompous shit about the vile alleys of the town being less murderous than the smiling face of the countryside. Mean, give me a break. What sort of shit is that?'

'As a matter of fact,' said Tudor priggishly, 'it's lifted straight from Sherlock Holmes. A short story called "The Copper Beeches" which is one of the *Adventures.* You can't get much more authentic than that.'

It was her turn to score a point.

'That's plagiarism,' she snarled. 'You're just ripping him off. In fact it's double plagiarism. You've nicked the names from Hardy and the dialogue from Conan Doyle. Why don't you try making up your own stuff? Do something original for a change.'

She was curled up on the sofa against the wall of Cornwall's office, showing a lot of leg, and breathing heavily. This made her seem disturbingly desirable. Cornwall, sitting in the high-backed leather chair behind his 1920s partners' desk, was not unmoved. The only light came from the anglepoise to the right of his computer screen. It cast a halo of yellow-gold making him look like a thin saint in some pre-Raphaelite painting.

'If it's to be a proper detective story it's got to have a proper detective,' he said.

'Who says?'

'I say. And the class agree.'

'I don't give a stuff about the class. Of course they agree. They want to get good marks and a decent degree. They're not going to get either by disagreeing.'

'That's not fair and you know it. You disagree about practically everything.'

'Which means I'm going to get straight alphas in everything?'

They looked at each other steadily, then both laughed.

'Seriously though,' he asked, 'what do you think?'

She shrugged. 'It doesn't matter what I think,' she said. 'I guess if you're turning the thing into a crime novel it'll just about do. Why Wintoncester by the way? You say Raleigh was tried there and King Arthur's table is hanging on the wall of the Great Hall so it has to be Winchester. Why not just say so?'

'Well,' he said. 'It is Winchester and it's not Winchester. It's modelled on the town but it's not a photographic image. Besides, it follows the Hardy convention, which incidentally he explains at some length in the introduction.'

'So it's the truth but not the exact truth?' She looked thoughtful, tugging at a wayward strand of long blonde hair.

'That's what fiction's all about, isn't it?' he said, sententiously.

'Life too,' she said. 'Everything in life is sort of true but it's not completely true. Truth, Whole Truth, nothing but the Truth, so help me God, but so help me God there's no such thing.'

'Same with death,' he said. 'We never know

54

for certain, do we? Even in an open-and-shut case like the D'Urberville murder.'

She squinted at him, and rearranged her legs in a way that came across as coquettish and might or might not have been intended to be so.

'Do you mean the fictional D'Urberville murder or the real life one?'

He smiled enigmatically. 'Not sure,' he said, 'at least not yet. I'm not even sure of the distinctions. One may be more true to life—or death—than the other, but I'm not sure which.'

CHAPTER SEVEN

Tudor addressed his class with a distinct lack of enthusiasm. Much of his mind was elsewhere, grappling with the real contemporary drama unfolding under the less than omniscient eye of Detective Chief Superintendent Trythall and the Wessex Constabulary. That part which was engaged with the group of students sprawled about the drab, functional lecture-room, was unenthusiastic, not so much about the subject under discussion, as with those who were supposed to be maintaining the other side of the argument. He knew perfectly well that they wanted his classes to be conducted as monologues in which they would be required to do nothing more than take a reasonably accurate note from which they would later be able to regurgitate a more or less accurate summary of what he had said, with no deviations let alone original input of their own. This was, by and large, the way that the good old U of W went about its business.

The university was almost Dickensian in its addiction to learning by rote and what Mr Gradgrind in *Hard Times* believed to be 'facts'. Tudor Cornwall was disposed to the view that there was no such thing as a 'fact' but he knew that this uncomfortable perception was unlikely to find favour with many of his fellow academics let alone with the student body. Elizabeth Burney was one the very few exceptions and the thought of her provoked a wry half-smile which surprised those of his students who were actually observing him.

'Now,' he repeated, in a voice intended to convey gravitas but which actually came across as the noise a man made when he had momentarily forgotten where he was and what he was supposed to be doing. Not that he was absent-minded in the usual conventional sense. Far from it. It was more that he was adroit at prioritization and clever at imagining that he was in the right place at the right time. And this was not it.

In his mind's eye he was not in this unattractive room with his unappealing class, he was on a murder hunt at dawn near Stonehenge in the company of armed police. Much more interesting.

'Now,' he repeated for a third time, aware that even those paying scant attention, would be beginning to think something was wrong, 'we have been studying the scene in which the police finally apprehend Tess in the belief that she is guilty of murder. Right?'

'Right,' they chorused. All but a few. Freddie, the Etonian, was staring at a book, open on his desk, and frowning.

Tudor assumed the book had nothing to do with the matter in hand and that Freddie was not paying attention.

Wrong. Freddie was capable of surprising one. You had to give him that.

'Do you think this stuff about sacrificing to the Sun rather than to God is significant?' he asked, and Tudor realized that the book he was frowning over was *Tess* and not, as he had believed, some cheap pulp fiction.

'What do you think, Freddie?' he asked, anxious as always to provoke something approximating to a dialogue.

'At the very end of the book Hardy says "the President of the Immortals has ended his sport with Tess",' said Freddie. 'The President of the Immortals is an ancient Greek concept. Aeschylus if Hardy's right. Not God, And not the Sun.'

'It's all like predetermined, yeah,' Spiky

Karl mumbled into his stubble.

'That's why it's not a whodunit,' said pretty Tamsin, unexpectedly.

'Come again,' said Tudor, surprising himself by beginning to take an interest in his pupils.

'Because God dunnit. Or the President of the Immortals,' she said. 'Even if Tess did kill Alec it's not her fault because she has no free will. She's just a toy to be played with.'

'That would be no defence in law,' said Tudor.

'But if the case were heard in Hardy's Wessex, you know, a fictitious country, like Greeneland is the world Graham Greene created, then the President of the Immortals, or God, or the Sun, or whatever is the author himself, then that might be a defence in law because the law would be like, well Hardy's law. Know what I mean?'

'Now steady on,' said Tudor, recognizing a discussion that was running away with itself. 'We have to accept, I think, that Hardy like most pre-Tolkien fantasists, is trying to present a world which is recognizably real. Then he inserts a story, characters and interpretations. He doesn't invent a world. He recreates it. It's his explanation which is the invention not the world itself.'

There was a silence in which you could almost hear the collective whirrings of cognitive apparatuses.

Tudor anticipated further trouble by

58

returning to basics.

'In what senses does the scene in the book differ from what one might expect to happen in modern times?'

Frances, the Geordie, put up a hand and didn't speak until he nodded at her.

'Stonehenge is an English Heritage site. In the book they just bump into the stones almost by accident. It's completely deserted. If you tried to kip on the altar, like Tess did, you'd be done for breaking and entering even if you got through the barbed wire and the Alsatians in the first place.'

The class tittered.

'Good scene though,' said Tudor. 'Dawn breaking. Angel Clare watching over his sleeping inamorata and then a circle of sixteen coppers surrounding them. It's as good in its way as the landlady looking up at the bleeding ceiling. That marvellous moment when the wind dies and "the stones lay still" and then, suddenly, something moves, just a dot, but it's a man in the distance, then another and another. Wearing helmets don't you think, though Hardy doesn't tell us that. And then they all gather round until she wakes and you have that brilliant final line: " 'I am ready,' she said quietly".'

'In a crime novel,' said Freddie, 'she'd have said "it's a fair cop"!'

Another collective class titter.

'If I'd been writing it I'd have been half-

59

inclined to call a halt there,' said Tudor. 'As it is, the rest of the book is, if you'll pardon the expression, "a bit of a cop-out". Don't you think?'

There was a collective shuffle, symptomatic of unease.

'You mean,' said Tamsin, 'that you'd finish with the arrest because we all know that she's guilty and the minute she's arrested the game's up and the story is finished.'

'You could put it like that,' said Tudor. 'All the final section of the book tells us is that Tess is hanged after a trial in which we presume she pleaded guilty and that Angel has gone off with her younger sister.'

'Which could be a motive.' This was Karl, the vegetarian pacifist.

'How do you mean?' asked Tudor, genuinely puzzled.

'If Angel had the hots for Liza-Lu but was married to her elder sister, then the only way he could get off with her would be to get Tess banged up, or better still, topped. So he frames her.'

'Sounds to me,' said Frances, 'as if Liza-Lu is under age. "Half girl, half woman—a spiritualized image of Tess, slighter than she, but with the same beautiful eyes". If you ask me Angel's just a creepy paedophile.'

'I certainly hadn't thought of him like that,' said Tudor truthfully, 'but there's another thing about that scene. It's all described from the point of view of Tess and Angel. They're looking out at the surrounding policemen. If it had been a crime novel we'd have seen it all from the point of view of Holmes and Watson, Father Brown, Wimsey, or Wexford, not the villain.'

'Are you calling Tess a villain?' Frances sounded personally affronted.

'If she really committed the murder then according to the conventions of the genre she's the villainess,' said Tudor.

'Unless you're Patricia Highsmith and you have a psychopathic hero like Ripley.' This was Karl, who was a Highsmith fan, inclined to identify with her complex amoral protagonist.

'The point I'm making is that Hardy clearly believes that Tess was the murderess but he also treats her as if she was a victim. In the classic crime story you can't do that. Classic crime is black and white and murderesses are black no matter how they're traduced and tempted and provoked and pressured. That's why the Victorians were so outraged by what Hardy wrote. They believed that a woman like Tess was an evil hussy. Hardy thought she was hard done by. You wouldn't have found Sir Arthur Conan Doyle poncing about like that. But . . .'

He looked around the class and was gratified to see that he had their attention.

'If Conan Doyle were writing the story he might well have wanted to sympathize with

Tess. He was a sympathetic sort of fellow. Civilized in a bluff, old-fashioned way. Would have seen that Tess had drawn a short straw and that D'Urberville was a cad and Angel a drip.'

The class nodded a collective assent.

'But,' he said, with thespian emphasis, 'if Conan Doyle or Crime Writer X wanted to come out for Tess, the only way that he could do it—in Victorian society—would be to demonstrate her innocence. He would have to make Sherlock Holmes and Dr Watson take up her case and confound Inspector Lestrade—who would almost certainly have been at the head of the "plods" who captured her on the altar at Stonehenge. My view is that if truth is to be served the Stonehenge scene has to be recorded from the point of view of the police or, more precisely, from the point of view of our detective—Tranter Reuben, man of leisure, friend and rival of Sherlock Holmes, one of the first of the great detectives. And his man Ledlow.'

The class seemed unconvinced and somehow impetus was lost and conversation dissipated. They broke up early and Tudor reverted to authorial mode. He wrote, therefore he solved. His was not just an academic discipline; it was creative too.

He visualized Stonehenge at dawn in the 1890s and wrote,

Tranter Reuben, Ledlow and the police fanned out and tramped across the plain. In the distance the henge emerged sinister in the light of the rising sun.

Or should it be setting moon? Was 'sinister' quite right? How 'distant' was 'distance'? Was 'henge' an acceptable variant of Stonehenge?

He sucked on his pencil, thought of those two concurrent genii, Hardy and Conan Doyle, and wrote some more.

The men advanced across the downland and turf as the night wind died, and the quivering little pools in the cup-like hollows of the stones lay still. Tranter turned up the collar of his coat against the early morning chill and contemplated their quarry. She was there, somewhere in the stones. He knew it.

From behind him, a few feet to his right, Ledlow, equally well muffled, coughed discreetly.

'Something moved,' he said, 'yonder. Near the Stone of Sacrifice.'

Tranter shaded his eyes with the palm of his hand and gazed towards the ancient columns of stones. Presently he too saw movement. There was a figure standing near the centre of the circle, seemingly casting about for something—a weapon perhaps. There was a prehensile quality to the movements. The figure reminded the detective of a wild animal who has just caught the scent of predatory hounds. He patted the reassuring bulk of his old service revolver. The police would be armed too. He sensed their prey would not be dangerous and yet a murder had been committed and the murderer would surely hang. There was nothing more dangerous than a cornered animal—confused, frightened, capable of anything. And yet he sensed the quarry would give no trouble.

For the next few minutes the encircling men trod purposefully across the frosty grass, like a human noose closing around an unprotected neck. Then suddenly they had penetrated the ring of stones and the first policeman laid a hand on the standing figure.

'It's no use sir,' he said, in the soft, reassuring tones of old Wessex, 'there are sixteen of us on the Plain, and the whole country is reared.'

The other man flinched from the policeman's grasp.

'Let her sleep,' he implored.

Only then did Tranter Reuben, Ledlow and the police see the sleeping form of a woman laid out on the sacrificial slab of the heathen temple. No one spoke but they gathered around in acquiescent silence, awed by the apparent innocence of the sleeping woman.

Presently it grew lighter until a ray from the sun shone upon her unconscious form.

'What is it, Angel?' she said, starting up. 'Have they come for me?'

Reuben was struck by the note of resignation in her voice. It was almost as if she had laid

64

herself out as a human sacrifice, waiting, vulnerable, for the hand of justice to apprehend her. But was it 'Justice'? Or was it 'Fate'?

'Yes, dearest,' he said, in a voice that Tranter instantly did not trust, 'they have come.'

'It is as it should be,' she murmured. 'Angel, I am almost glad—yes, glad! This could not have lasted. It was too much. I have had enough; and now I shall not live for you to despise me!'

She stood up, shook herself and went forward. 'I am ready,' she said quietly.

Tranter Reuben could sense the certainty in the mind of each one of the sixteen policemen, and even, bless him, of simple Ledlow at his side. In their eyes the case was solved, the crime was closed.

But Tranter Reuben believed no such thing. No matter that the world believed in Tess's guilt; no matter that she herself confessed her crime.

Tranter Reuben knew, deep in his bones, that an injustice was on the verge of being done.

Tudor Cornwall laid down his pencil and read through what he had written. It wasn't quite right. He knew that. Little Elizabeth Burney would tear it to shreds. Yet the more he thought and the more that he wrote the more he knew, as certainly as Tranter Reuben the great detective, that Tess of the D'Urbervilles had not done it.

CHAPTER EIGHT

In real life Tudor rode shotgun to Stonehenge.

Eddie Trythall was predictably but quite reasonably sceptical about the enterprise. However, as Tudor pointed out, his men had proved singularly useless at finding Mrs D'Urberville or whoever she was. The woman had vanished. Tudor did not add 'into thin air' but 'thin air' seemed to be what had become of her. It was as if she had never been.

Tudor was something of an expert on disappearance. His paper—'The Lady Vanishes—Dame Agatha, Lord Lucan and others'—was highly regarded in the world of criminal academe, to such an extent that he was seriously considering turning it into a book. One or two publishers had been sniffing around his agent, but most of them wanted something more sensational. He was amazed at how many otherwise quite normal people believed that such prominent victims of unexpected accidents such as Robert Maxwell and Diana, Princess of Wales were still alive and well with new appearances and identities. One senior editor at an Anglo-American publisher actually told him as a certain fact that Maxwell was running the Israeli Intelligence Agency, Mossad. No one in publishing or newspapers appeared to believe that the body buried on a small island at the Spencers' ancestral home was actually that of Diana. Most people seemed to think the Althorp coffin was empty and that Diana was alive and well in Paraguay. And so on.

Tudor did not subscribe to this nonsense but he did believe that it was at least as possible to stage a vanishing trick in metropolitan Britain as it was in the Tasmanian bush. His former friend, Professor Ashley Carpenter, had managed it in the bush; now this latter day Tess seemed to have pulled off something similar in urban England.

He wasn't surprised.

'I still think this is bloody ridiculous,' said Eddie Trythall as their unmarked police car drove north through the early Wiltshire morning. It was frosty but fine, crisp with a sky edged in pink and gold but turning Cambridge blue.

'Got a better idea?' asked Tudor, grinning. He knew his old friend and sparring partner had run out of inspiration.

The policeman made no reply. Publicly he invariably said that his chaps, like the Mounties, always got their man. Privately he knew that their failure rate was unacceptable, that they were unable to secure as many convictions as they should and that, disturbingly often, they were unable to find people who did not wish to be found. Tudor, exasperatingly, argued that, in a democratic free society the citizen had a perfect right to disappear if he had committed no crime. Tudor recognized that many people had good reason for opting out of life as they knew it and if that's what they wanted then why not? Eddie, however, was like most policemen. He might not have quite been a control freak but he certainly wasn't a libertarian. He liked regular roll-calls, needed to know that all were present and correct. Sir.

'In the book,' said Tudor, knowing that this would provoke the chief superintendent, 'they holed up in a deserted house. Did a squat. Got away with it for a day or two. They were heading north, making for an unexpected port. But Tess got tired so they kipped at Stonehenge. Well, *she* did. Angel seems to have stayed up most of the night. It was a ludicrous place to stop. One of the most exposed and visible spots in the whole of England. It was almost as if they were willing themselves to be caught.'

'Still *is* exposed and visible,' said Trythall morosely. 'Why in God's name would someone on the run hide away at Wiltshire's biggest tourist attraction?'

'Crowds make good hiding-places. Isn't that basic field-craft?'

'If you say so.' Trythall was tetchy. 'Though what an ivory-tower dweller like yourself would know about basic field-craft, God alone knows.'

Tudor ignored the barb.

'That's a piece of Devil's advocacy,' he said. 'The original Angel and Tess weren't trying to escape. Not really. Tess didn't even make a pretence of it. She'd had enough. She saw herself as a human sacrifice. Why else did she sleep out on the altar? It's all symbolic. She wanted out.'

'And Clare?'

'My belief,' said Tudor, 'is that Clare is a fraud and a sham and quite possibly the real villain of the piece. If he'd really wanted to escape he wouldn't have ended up at Stonehenge. He tried to persuade Tess to carry on and find somewhere safer but he doesn't make much of a job of it. He's just going through the motions.'

Stonehenge was in sight now. Tudor could quote chunks of Hardy: '*The eastward pillars and their architraves stood up blackly against the light, and the great flame-shaped Sun-stone beyond them; and the Stone of Sacrifice midway.*' In the light of day the ancient temple had become a victim of modern tourism, sanitized and reduced by the baleful influence of English Heritage, renowned primarily as an impediment to necessary improvements to the arterial A303 London to Exeter highway. The plan was to build a visitors' centre. This would eliminate wear and tear to the real thing. Already the public were cordoned off so that they could not, as they had a hundred years or so earlier, walk among the sinister stones much less stretch out and sleep on the Stone of Sacrifice. In future the original monument would take second place to an artificial rival. The fake Stonehenge would be better lit, better displayed, more accessible than the real one. Now in the crepuscular aftermath of dawn the standing stones maintained some of their former strength and menace. Tudor shuddered slightly. The stones seemed baleful, oozing with animal threat. They exuded something primitive and dangerous which vanished with daylight and coachloads of trippers.

The car's headlights illuminated a confusing and unsightly signpost indicating the whereabouts of car-parks, and coach-parks, urinals, creches, disabled facilities, food and beverage points, ticket offices and all the other necessaries of modern tourism. It was a far cry, thought Tudor, from Druids and human sacrifice.

They pulled up in the first car-park alongside a police van from which there emerged a dozen or so uniformed police, two of them with lean and hungry-looking German Shepherds on leashes. Tudor thought sadly of the forlorn woman they were seeking and wondered why even a relatively sophisticated copper like Eddie Trythall always seemed to take sledgehammers to nuts. There surely was no need for this. It was like bringing the Rapid

Response Squad in to deal with a fare dodger. It made him angry on several counts, not least because he knew that elsewhere when strength was required it wasn't there—to deal with Saturday Night and Sunday Morning in Sandbourne, for instance, particularly when Athletic had a home game against a team like Millwall. He had made this point repeatedly at crime conferences where academics such as himself came up against the police.

The police response, with a few exceptions of whom Eddie Trythall was often one, was maddeningly similar.

'It's all very well for you academics,' they would say. 'You've never been a bobby on the beat; you've never been shot at or stabbed. You're nothing but hot air and academic papers. That's fine—you theorize as much as you like but leave proper policing to the grown-ups.'

'Expecting some sort of riot are we?' Tudor asked sarcastically, turning from the platoon of police to the virtual emptiness of the enormous car-park. Across the road the stones, cordoned off from the vulgar herd, stared back implacably.

'I thought there was no overnight parking allowed,' he continued, nodding to a far corner of the park where what looked like a pre-war omnibus cowered in the gloaming. A dog barked and Tudor saw that there was an Alsatian on the end of a long rope tied to the

71

bus's door. Even in the half-light and from this distance it had a badly bred, ill-fed appearance which contrasted unhappily with that of its police counterparts.

'There's an understanding about travellers,' said Trythall. 'They come for the solstice. There are so many that they're beyond proper control so we've come to an agreement. It's effectively a sort of self-policing agreement. We turn a blind eye to cannabis provided they don't do heroin and stuff, at least in public; we tolerate a certain amount of rowdiness provided it isn't allowed to degenerate into something life-threatening. And so on. Live and let live. It's an acceptance of reality.'

'A sort of occasional travelling no-go area?' Tudor was unimpressed.

'If you put it like that,' said Eddie watching his subordinates fan out under the supervision of one of his inspectors. They looked as if they were searching for a body rather than a living person. Their eyes were fixed on the ground immediately in front of them rather than scanning the horizon or even middle distance.

'So what's he doing here?'

Tudor nodded in the direction of the dilapidated old charabanc and the emaciated Alsatian.

'God knows,' said Eddie. 'Waiting for the winter solstice perhaps?'

'Which isn't for another six weeks or more,' said Tudor.

72

'I don't know,' said Eddie. 'Like I said, the drill here is that provided travellers keep their noses clean, and there aren't too many, the authorities turn a blind eye. He's probably, just, you know, travelling.'

Tudor smiled thinly.

'Why don't you and I go and take a look?' he said. The inhabitants of the police van had set off in line abreast as if beating for game birds. They were heading away from the old bus.

Eddie Trythall shrugged.

'If you like,' he said. 'One wild goose chase on top of another.'

So they set off together towards the far corner of the park. The policeman's metal toe and heel caps beat out a steady staccato pattern on the tarmac while the academic's brothel-creeping desert boots scarcely sounded a shuffle. A truck changed gear at the roundabout on the A303 and accelerated west towards Somerset and Dorset. A motor bike passed in the other direction and vanished towards Amesbury. Then there was nothing from the road. It was still early for traffic.

As they neared the bus, the dog started to snarl and strain at its rope. Inside the vehicle a light snapped on, and a man's voice irritably, called out in what sounded like Mockney with a trace of brogue, 'Dolly, shut your noise!'

Dolly did nothing of the kind but continued to bare teeth and make canine noises halfway

73

between threat and fear.

Presently there were noises off, the front door of the bus was opened and a man stood silhouetted on the step down from the cab. He was about 5' 10", skinny, stubbled, thirty-something and with a ring through his lip and another through his left nostril. His hair was greased and spiky. He wore scruffy jeans, Doc Martens, an off-white T-shirt and a pseudo-leather jacket with a skull and crossbones above the heart and the legend Angel Clare picked out in studs.

'Is that your name?' asked Tudor, metaphorically pinching himself.

'No it effing isn't!' The brogue was more pronounced now. 'I'm an effing Hell's Angel and I'm from the effing County Clare chapter. What kept you, you bastards? You should have been here days ago. That's what Al told us. One of you must be Inspector Trythall and the other's Professor Cornwall. And you're effing late. Another twenty-four hours and we'd have moved the shite on.'

'Chief Superintendent Trythall and Doctor Cornwall,' said Tudor, wishing he didn't always sound prissy in moments of stress. 'We've come for Tess. Mrs D'Urberville.'

'Don't patronize me, sunshine,' said the Angel. 'I know who you've bleeding come for. She's asleep and if you know what's good for you, you'll let her finish her kip.'

Tudor frowned. A century or so ago the

fugitive would have been laid out on the sacrificial slab not dossed down in a traveller's clapped out omnibus. And her protector would have been a soft-spoken gentle man who would have implored them in a whisper, not threatened them with a rant. Time, reflected Tudor, had wrought some strange changes.

'We have no objection,' he said, glancing at his friend, who nodded.

And he remembered the words of the great novelist.

All waited in the growing light, their faces and hands as if they were silvered, the remainder of their figures dark, the stones glistening green gray, the Plain still a mass of shade.

And as he waited he reflected that he felt much the same about the Angel before him as he did about the Angel in the book.

Feeling this he shivered once more and not just from the cold in the bitter morning air.

CHAPTER NINE

The interior of the bus was crummy.

Some time, fifty years earlier, it must have been state of the art. You could imagine Preston North End using it to travel to Blackpool for a First Division match starring Tom Finney and Stanley Matthews. A well-heeled Women's Institute might have travelled to London in it for the Coronation. The driver would have worn a peaked cap and a jacket and tie.

Now, however, it smelt of stale bodies, canine and human; of last night's cigarettes and cheap liquor. Threadbare blankets made do for curtains and there were armchairs of fake brown leather with broken springs for sitting on. Baked-bean cans, open and half consumed, sat on the shelves along with over-flowing ashtrays and greasy plates.

This, thought Tudor, is how the other half lives. No, that was wrong. This was the bottom ten per cent, surely. In the civilized west at any rate. Surely nine-tenths of the population would have thought it squalid?

He hoped so.

Presently there was movement from behind a hanging blanket and a woman emerged. She wore what looked like an old RAF officer's blue-grey greatcoat which came down to her ankles and was tied at the waist with a bright yellow braided rope. Her hair was limp and greasy, her eyes were bleary and when she rubbed at them with her hands, the sleeves of her coat fell back to reveal a serpentine tattoo on her right forearm.

'So they come at last,' she said, to her companion; and then, 'Got a fag, darling?'

No one spoke as the biker found a cheap cigarette and lit it for her, using an old-fashioned Zippo lighter which flared up alarmingly as he raspingly spun the fly-wheel. She inhaled deeply and blew blue smoke out of her nostrils which, slightly to Tudor's surprise, were unpierced and unadorned. She could have been pretty in a waif-like way if she hadn't appeared so emaciated and unwell. A hundred years ago you'd have said she was consumptive. In the modern world you'd assume she was HIV positive.

'I'm ready,' she said eventually, looking up at Tudor and Eddie from under lowered lashes.

'Don't you want to pack some things?' asked Tudor. He felt solicitous. She seemed young enough to be his daughter even if she wasn't. Whatever she'd done, whatever she was, he could not but be touched by her vulnerability.

'I travel light,' she said, 'always have.'

'You may not be coming back,' said Eddie Trythall. 'If things work out the way I think they're going to, you'll be out of circulation for

77

quite a while.'

'Don't pussyfoot with me,' she said, 'you mean remanded in custody, open-and-shut trial, guilty verdict, life sentence. Years not months. But I'll have a roof over my head, food to eat, clothes to wear, female company. Make a change, I can tell you. You ever been on the run, on the road? No joke, specially in this weather. No thank you, I've no need to pack anything.'

'Tell you what,' said Tudor, anxious to be conciliatory, 'I'm sure my friend Superintendent Trythall would like a word in private with Irish Biker here. Why don't I walk you over to the cafeteria and stand you breakfast while the other two sort some things out.'

'I don't do breakfast,' she said, sulkily.

'Well, coffee then.'

The woman looked mulish, then shrugged acquiescence. Tudor felt she didn't care.

'If you like,' she said.

'I do like,' he said. 'But I'm only trying to be helpful.'

'That's not your style from what I hear.'

He gave her a sharp look, trying to penetrate the schoolgirl pout.

'What exactly do you mean by that?' he asked.

'Nothing,' she said, making it sound as if she had said 'nuffink'. He felt like clipping her round the ears, rather as one or two of the more old-fashioned teachers had done to him when he was at school. He resisted the urge but he recognized potential temper loss. She was reminding him of some of his students; the ones who sat at the back of his class and complained that it was difficult to take notes from him. He metaphorically pinched himself. She was a suspected murderess on the run, dammit. He should treat her as such, though to be frank his first-hand experience of such people was non-existent. He had plenty of vicarious knowledge but he had to acknowledge, privately, that Eddie's distinction between himself at the sharp end and cutting edge and Tudor, locked in the abstract theory of the ivory tower had moments of truth. Eddie was used to the front line; Tudor was one of nature's staff officers.

'Come on,' he said, roughly, 'coffee.'

She shrugged but came with him out of the bus and into crisp morning daylight. In the distance, Tudor could see the line of uniformed police trudging stolidly across the Plain. Trythall should have told them to stop because the game was up. Tudor thought of interfering and decided against. It was none of his business and the exercise would do them good. They could treat it as training, write it down to experience.

Beside him the woman coughed a rattling, mucous-charged smoker's cough and dropped her fag-end on the tarmac. Part of Tudor wanted to make her pick it up and put it in a bin. A better part said nothing, just paced out towards the cafeteria signs. A few steps across the car-park and he realized she was wearing slippers over bare feet. Tartan ones, threadbare as the old blankets that draped the bus windows.

'You must be cold,' he said, and sensed rather than saw the shrug which greeted the pleasantry. This wasn't the time for small talk. Eddie would have known that.

He said nothing more until they reached the door of the cafeteria which, of course, was locked. Inside, the neon lights were on and Tudor could see staff in aprons and health-and-safety regulation headgear sitting about and hoping against hope that this would be the first day in the history of the place when no visitors wanted food or drink.

Tudor rapped on the glass. No one looked up. He rapped louder. Still nothing.

'They're closed,' she said. 'It's only just seven. It's another hour till opening time—if we're lucky.'

Tudor swore under his breath and banged a third time even louder. A blank-faced, middle-aged woman who gave the impression of being in some sort of charge, got up slowly, walked to the door and pointed to the closed sign. Then she held up the wrist with the watch on it and pointed pantomime-fashion to the figure eight. Tudor responded in similar mime designed to suggest extreme cold, thirst and general distress not so much in himself but the damsel beside him. The woman looked at Tess or whatever she was calling herself, grimaced and opened the door.

'We're not open for another hour,' she said.

'But,' said Tudor, pleadingly, 'she's not at all well. All we want's a coffee. We'll sit quiet in a corner. You can lock the door behind us. We'll pretend we're staff.'

'I know she's not well, poor lass,' said the supervisor, suddenly becoming almost human. 'All right, as it's her. But don't tell anyone. And sit over there, round the corner where no one can see. Otherwise there'll be mayhem.'

Mayhem seemed an unlikely eventuality in this empty place at this godless hour, but Tudor smiled as if gangs of rioters might burst in at any moment, and allowed himself and his companion to be shepherded conspiratorially to a dark and obscure corner of the hall. There they settled themselves on opposite sides of a formica-topped table. Tudor watched as she searched in the pockets of the greatcoat and finally extricated a packet of Woodbines and a box of matches.

The supervisor came to them with a couple of mugs of hot brown liquid just as the Woodbine started to burn.

'There's no smoking,' she said.

The suspected murderess paid no attention, inhaled, exhaled and coughed alarmingly.

Tudor gazed at her sorrowfully and supposed that if you had just killed your man and were being arrested for it you weren't going to be bothered about petty restrictions on smoking in public places. Particularly if you seemed to be at death's door.

'Didn't your mother tell you it's rude to stare?' she said, staring back at him.

'I said there's no smoking,' said the supervisor 'You'll have to leave.'

'What the fuck,' said the accused.

'She's under a lot of strain,' said Tudor, doing his best to be charming, distressed and masterful all in one breath. It seemed to have the desired effect. The bringer of coffee's expression was halfway between compassion and disdain, but she obviously thought the easiest course of action was mistressly inactivity. Story of her life, thought Tudor, as she flounced back to her dawdling colleagues, muttering as she went.

There was a plastic tomato on the table, its green stalk smeared with ketchup. Also a sugar dispenser and a salt-cellar with no salt in it.

'What's your real name?' Tudor asked her, more for want of anything to say than from genuine curiosity.

'What do you mean "real"?' she wanted to know.

Tudor felt pulled up short. No one had ever responded quite like that. Mind you, no one nowadays asked questions in quite such a

82

forthright manner. When it came to names he found that most interlocutors, usually anonymous voices on the telephone, asked him to 'confirm' his name. For a while, in a donnish manner, he had answered them by saying, 'Certainly, you tell me what you think it is and I'll confirm it.' This was always regarded as unhelpful and invariably met with 'Don't get smart with me, Mr Cornwall, just confirm your name to me', and he would say, 'Now you've told me what you think it is I'm happy to confirm that you're absolutely right'. This always led to further confusion and ill-feeling so he resolved to stop trying to educate people and take the easy way out by telling them what they wanted to hear. That way lay tin-pot dictatorship. He knew it but, really, he couldn't be bothered. Life was too short He knew it was lazy and that it was the duty of people like him to stand up for what they believed in, even if was only the correct use of English.

'What do I mean by *real*,' he said, 'that's a question of metaphysics rather than nomenclature. What I mean to say is what do you usually call yourself?'

'Depends what you mean by usually,' she said.

He sipped some dark-brown stuff. It could have been anything really: instant Windsor brown soup, gravy, warm Vegemite. They had asked for coffee, she had said it was coffee, did that make it coffee? Oh dear. More metaphysics.

'You know what I mean,' he said, rising awkwardly to the challenge.

'Maybe,' she said, 'maybe not.'

Christ, he thought to himself, if she was always like that he was amazed she had killed D'Urberville and not the other way round. He already felt like throttling her.

'If you must know,' she said, dropping the adversarial pose almost as quickly as she had adopted it, 'I've had so many different names I don't really know which is real and which isn't. And I'm not sure what's real anyway. Alec did that for me. His analysts said he had a very precarious grip on reality but Al used to say to me that you couldn't have a firm grip on something that didn't exist.'

'What did he call you?'

She took a sip of the liquid and winced, though Tudor wasn't sure whether because of the heat or the flavour.

'Depends,' she said. 'Tess recently. Tessie. Tessa. Darling. Dearest. Mrs D'Urberville. Lady D'Urberville. He didn't like to call me the same name too many times. He said it got boring.'

He returned to the first question. 'When I say *real* name I suppose I mean the name you were christened with: the name your mother gave you.'

She laughed if you could call such a

84

dispirited, joyless expression by such a gay word as 'laugh'.

'For a start I was never christened. My mum wouldn't have known what that meant. And she gave me all kinds of names, not many of them very nice. When she was in company she called me Kate. That was *her* mum's name. I think she loved her which is more than she ever did me.' She stubbed the butt of her cigarette into the side of the plastic tomato and twisted it viciously. There was smell of burning plastic.

'But like I said I've had more names than I can remember. Same as Al.'

'Al?'

'Al,' she said. 'My husband. Al. Alex. Alec. Alexander. Was Albert once. Alfred too. So Bert and Fred when it suited. You're never the same person very long in the sort of world I live in. But you wouldn't know about that. You don't have the first idea of what it's like down here, you really don't.'

She was right. He knew that. It was what Eddie Trythall always said, but Eddie didn't know either. Eddie had a salary, security, a roof over his head, a pension waiting. This woman, her biker friend, her dead husband, they had nothing. It didn't matter how well you understood it intellectually, there was no way you could understand it emotionally, viscerally, in your gut.

'Did you kill him?'

The blunt question surprised him even more than it seemed to surprise her. He had hardly known he was going to ask it. It was involuntary.

She looked at him steadily for a few moments, then smiled, though with no more joy than when she had laughed.

'If I said yes you wouldn't believe me. If I said no you wouldn't believe me. So just for now I'm saying nothing.' That word came out like 'nuffink' again. She took another swig of liquid and winced again.

'I have had enough,' she said, then assumed what Tudor supposed was her version of a posh accent. 'And now I shall not live for you to despise me.'

'That's what Tess said,' said Tudor, shocked, 'in the book.'

She laughed again and looked him hard in the eyes.

'Yes,' she said, and then quietly, 'I am ready.'

'That too,' said Tudor.

'Yes,' she said, 'that too.'

CHAPTER TEN

Later in the day Eddie and Tudor adjourned to the Imperial and the policeman gave his friend a book.

The dead man's copy of *Tess of the D'Urbervilles*, was a study in compulsive obsession. Smith alias D'Urberville had been fourteen when he won the book as a prize during his second year at Osmington, the very, very minor public school from which his mother removed him at the time of his father's death.

This sudden end of formal education had obviously, well probably, had a traumatic effect on a child who was academically promising, at least when it came to English Literature. The book was a Collins edition published in 1958, and printed and bound by Hartnolls Limited of Bodmin, Cornwall. For some reason the prize-winner had circled the word 'Cornwall' in green ink. Then, when the text proper began, the underlinings and circlings and exclamation marks gathered strength until on some pages there was almost more of the owner than the author. On page 28, for example, the second page of the story, there was a paragraph in which Parson Tringham, the antiquary of Stagfoot Lane, explains to drunken old Durbeyfield, Tess's dad, that he comes from ancient and noble stock, being descended from one of the twelve knights who *assisted the Lord of Estremavilla in his conquest of Glamorganshire.* There follows a brief dissertation on the genealogy of the Durbeyfields or D'Urbervilles, rather in the manner of Sellar and Yeatman in *1066 and All That* with lines such as, *In Edward the Second's time your forefather Brian was summoned to Westminster to attend the great council there.* That particular line, reflected Cornwall, was more like Monty Python than Sellar and Yeatman.

In any event it had prompted the owner to scribble, irritably, in a spidery, backward-sloping hand, *Normans, Plantagenets, Stuarts, the Protectorate even, but no Tudors.* Each dynasty was in a different colour so that the Normans were green, the Plantagenets blue, the Stuarts yellow, Cromwell pencil grey, and the Tudors red.

This rainbow effect was maintained throughout the book's 448 pages. They were dog-eared and grubby through much handling and there was not a page that had escaped the owner's annotation. Sometimes words were underlined, sometimes ringed, occasionally there were exclamation marks, occasionally question marks, from time to time single words such as 'balls' or 'exactly'. Once or twice there were phrases or sentences. Tudor noticed 'Alec nicer than Hardy makes out', 'Tess mad, bad or just sad?', 'Angel no angel'. It looked at first glance as if Smith's interpretation was relentlessly masculine in the old-fashioned Victorian sense of regarding Tess as no more than 'a little harlot who probably led poor Alec on'. His may have been an interpretation that the author would have rejected but it looked as if he believed Alec to be the hero and Tess the villain of the piece.

Cornwall spent several minutes turning the pages, marvelling at the dedication which had produced so many readings and so many multi-coloured squiggles.

'I can't help feeling,' he said, eventually, 'that the answer's here.'

Eddie Trythall sighed.

'I thought you'd say that,' he said, sipping a lukewarm cup of the hotel's vile tea. 'What answer exactly? And what's the question?'

'The question's "whodunnit",' said Tudor irritably. 'I don't know what the answer is. I need to study the book.'

'Why bother to study the book when you've got such an obvious suspect?'

'Because,' said Cornwall, as if patronizing a dim pupil in a one-to-one tutorial, 'the obvious solution is too bloody obvious. Just as it is in the book. Hardy is completely unquestioning. He takes everything at face value. He asks no questions.'

Eddie Trythall picked a tea-leaf from a mildly discoloured front tooth.

'He's only the author, not the effing detective,' he said.

Tudor pressed his fingers together and held them thoughtfully under his nose. It was a characteristic pose designed to stall speech from anyone else and to give the impression that Tudor was thinking something profound. Eventually he broke the silence.

'Look,' he said, 'on the face of it I grant you the case is a grubby little domestic with an obvious culprit, but'—and here he frowned again over the fingers raised to his face, almost as if in prayer—'there are some very odd coincidences.'

'Coincidence,' said Trythall, 'suggests chance. I don't think there's anything coincidental about this. I think our corpse took the name Alec D'Urberville knowing perfectly well what he was doing. He didn't just happen to call himself Alec D'Urberville. It wasn't a name he plucked out of thin air. It wasn't even a name he happened to find in the phone book. It was a name which was central to this book which he won as a prize at school. It was obviously a book which was important in his life. I don't argue with any of this, but I have to ask myself whether it has any bearing on the crime I'm investigating. At the moment I don't see that it does. This bloke—Smith, D'Urberville, call him what you like—was a small-time thief, conman and general loser with no recognizable sense of morality. He had a row with his wife, girl-friend, partner or whatever, and she stabbed him with a knife causing death. In France they'd call it *a crime passionel.* We call it a domestic. No mystery. No romance. No factor to raise it above the everyday, boring, mundane, routine, sordid little killing my colleagues and I have to deal with several times every year. So help me God.'

He picked up a triangular cucumber sandwich, regarded it distastefully, and returned it to the plate.

Cornwall thought to himself that his old friend probably treated suspects a bit like that—stale cucumber sandwiches to be raked over with a sceptical stare and either unenthusiastically devoured or returned to the plate. Even as he thought it, he recognized that he was being academically whimsical. Criminal suspects, particularly those suspected of murder, could hardly be compared with cucumber sandwiches even in the rarified atmosphere of the ivory tower or the lecture hall. That way madness lies.

'Not many of your murder victims choose aliases from great English novels,' he said. 'Nor end up dying in the same way and much the same place. And the fact that a much-thumbed and obsessively annotated copy of the same great English novel is found among the dead man's very meagre personal effects adds to the oddity. Wouldn't you agree?'

The detective looked at the tired cucumber sandwich as if he might subject it to a further cross-examination, but thought better of it.

'He wasn't stupid, you know,' he said morosely.

The Garden Lounge of the Imperial Hotel, Sandbourne, was growing dim in the wintery afternoon. Waiters, neither hot nor cold, in their Laodicean indifference, drifted listlessly to and fro in the gloaming, human echoes of the cucumber sandwiches.

'Excuse me,' said Cornwall, to a sallow one of their number, as he shuffled past, 'would you mind turning a light on? And bring another pot of tea?'

It was on the tip of his tongue to suggest a fresh cucumber sandwich but he realized as the request was on the tip of his tongue that this would have been an oxymoronic request.

'Actually,' said Cornwall, in response to his old friend's judgement, 'I'd say he was better than not stupid. I'd say he was quite bright. Warped maybe, but bright.'

'Slipped through the net,' said the superintendent. 'Could have been a senior policeman or even a university lecturer if he'd had the education.'

'Instead of which,' said Cornwall, 'he *was* what he was—a waste of space. Worse than that. He was a positive force for bad, a habitual criminal, nasty piece of work, threat to the rest of us hard-working, honest, life-enhancing, socially aware decent folk.'

'That's a pretty Poujadist sentiment,' said Trythall. Just because the policeman was largely self-educated didn't mean to say that he wasn't educated at all. Rather the reverse. Unlike Cornwall whose erudition was essentially conventional and conditioned by a core curriculum and concomitant exam requirements, he occasionally came up with the wholly unexpected. 'Sort of thing.' he went on, 'that you'd expect from a *Daily Telegraph* reader.'

Cornwall who was an *Independent* or *Guardian* man coloured in response to the obvious insult.

'I don't see that believing in original sin is a middle-class offence,' he said. 'I think our man Smith was flawed from the off. One of nature's bad apples. He'd have been a villain no matter what.'

'Nature not nurture?'

'If you put it like that,' Cornwall nodded.

'Bound to come to a sticky end?' Trythall was doing dog-with-bone.

'Not necessarily,' said Cornwall. 'You could even argue the reverse. The world we live in may not favour the out-and-out law-breaker but it's certainly geared towards the amoral, the greedy, the chancer. Do you really believe you could run a prosperous business let alone a profitable bank if you were a good man within the meaning of the act?'

'Would you push it that far?'

Cornwall pressed his fingers together in that prayerful gesture of his and was silent for a moment.

'I think I probably would,' he said after a while. 'It's not a new phenomenon. Old as the Bible, maybe older. Rich-man-going-through-eye-of-needle stuff. You can't succeed in our world without being fundamentally unpleasant.'

'But Smith alias D'Urberville was nasty and a failure.'

Cornwall smiled thinly over his hands.

'Smith alias D'Urberville,' he said, 'was nasty enough but not very good at it.'

A waiter with lank black hair and dandruff on the reveres of his frayed but gilded frock coat brought a new pot and Cornwall played Mum and poured.

They both sipped regretfully, not enjoying it, but feeling somehow obliged to by the afternoon-tea ambience of their surroundings.

Cornwall put down his cup and picked up the copy of *Tess*, flipping through its heavily annotated pages.

'We're not much further on,' he said.

'No,' agreed Trythall. 'But I thought you'd be interested in the book.'

'I am,' said Cornwall. 'Talking of the Bible, do you think this was his?'

'Meaning?'

'Meaning just that.' Cornwall was thinking out loud. 'That this was the book by which he lived. His rule book, if you like. A devout Christian would read the Bible every day and act accordingly; a Muslim, the Koran; a Communist, Marx, for all I know. This guy was just like any other religious fundamentalist only his beliefs were based on *Tess of the D'Urbervilles* by Thomas Hardy.'

'A Hardyist or a D'Urbervillite?' Trythall

94

was mocking him.

'No more absurd than being a Ranter or a Muggletonian,' said Cornwall, who had not read Modern History for nothing.

'This is the twenty-first century,' riposted the policeman.

'Which,' said Cornwall, 'is at least as full of batty beliefs as the seventeenth. I'd say people are even more gullible and susceptible now than they were then. And there are at least as many bogus high priests to lead them on. And with unprecedented weapons of mass persuasion at their disposal.'

'But our man was a solitary. He wasn't an evangelist or a member of a sect. He was a one-off.'

'Hermit of Peking. The Baptist in the Wilderness.' Cornwall sipped more tea and puckered his lips. 'Doesn't make it any less plausible. We live in an age of great loneliness. Modern man is solitary in the crowd, wouldn't you say?'

'Perhaps.' The Detective Chief Superintendent sipped tea as if in tacit agreement. There was much loneliness in the Garden Lounge of the Imperial: elderly couples simmering with irritated non-communication, old ladies with dogs or paid human companions, gentlemen hosts strayed from superannuated cruise-liners gliding like old Ivor Novellos through weekly *thé dansants.*

'But,' said Trythall, wiping his upper lip with

brisk efficiency, 'at the end of the day our man Smith or D'Urberville or whoever, is the victim not the perpetrator. So whatever he was getting from this book is neither here nor there.'

'Perhaps, perhaps not,' said Cornwall gnomically, irritating Trythall with this evasive even-mindedness. Policemen, reflected Trythall, could not afford the equivalences of academe. They were judged by results. It was the arriving that mattered for people such as him, not the getting there. Almost the exact opposite of what universities were about.

They sat silent in the gloom, punctuated now by the light from the occasional incomplete chandelier, until presently Tudor, for it was his shout, called for the bill and paid.

'If you don't mind,' he said, 'I'll hang on to the book for a day or so. I'd like a proper look and there's someone in particular I'd like to share it with.'

'It's all yours,' said Trythall. As soon as I opened it I thought, this is one for Tudor. Of academic interest only.'

Cornwall smiled.

'Of academic interest certainly,' he said. 'Of academic interest only . . . well, let's just say we'll see, shall we?'

CHAPTER ELEVEN

'This week's tutorial is a walk,' said Tudor. 'It'll probably rain so bring your Driza-bone. What sort of boots do you have?'

There was an Antipodean snigger across the ether from Elizabeth Burney's mobile to his. He wondered idly and vaguely where she was. That was one of the problems with the mobile. In the old days of fixed land-line phones you could put a trace on the call and work out exactly where the other half of the conversation was talking from. You made arrests like that in black and white Rank movies. Not any more. The mobile made one elusive, invisible even. It made it possible to reconcile disappearance with accessibility—as he knew to his cost.

'R. M. Williams,' she said, 'like all good Aussie girls and boys.'

'Williams make dry-weather boots,' said Tudor, with the authority of a man who had a pair himself. 'It will be wet. There will be mud and slurry. We won't go unduly far so you'd be best off with old fashioned wellies. Preferably not green. Try the Army and Navy in Troy Street.'

Another snigger.

When she did turn up for the walking tutorial she was in Driza-bone, waterproof

Akubra-style hat and a pair of dark-blue wellington gumboots purchased on sale at the Army and Navy.

'Both fetching and sensible,' said Tudor, who was in belted riding mac, tweed cap and brown well-dubbined leather boots that looked like army issue from World War Two. His trousers were sensible brown cords, the bottoms stuck into thick, equally sensible, red walking socks. Teacher and student looked, as they were, virtual stereotypes of the outdoor Sheila and the outdoor Pom.

'We'll take the car,' he said, his Morgan, British racing green, second-hand, manual gears and steering, leaky, shaky was the car of choice for a certain sort of middle-aged, tweedy English bloke. Morgan drivers tended to be trying to recover lost youth. The car looked raffish, exciting, uncomfortable. Tudor loved it. He called her Daphne and she not only made him feel young, she allowed him escape and relaxation, abandonment even.

They drove north to a point west of Cerne Abbas otherwise known as Abbot's Cernel.

'I wanted us to discuss "place",' he said, as the car throbbed along the greasy lanes. 'Place is important in crime especially crime fiction. Think Dartmoor in *Hound of the Baskervilles.* Think Oxford in Colin Dexter. Think Chicago for Sara Paretsky; Detroit for Loren Estelman. The place is almost more important than the plot. And even though we don't class him as a crime writer Hardy's strong on place, too. You could argue that Hardy's countryside is the most important character in his books. And yet he's peculiar, too. Remember that passage in the 1895 Preface to *Tess?* The bit where he explains why he calls Bulbarrow and the Devil's Kitchen and Stonehenge by their real names but changes Sherborne to Sherton Abbas and Winchester to Wintoncester?'

The girl shut her eyes, put her head back and recited from memory, *'It may be well to state, in response to enquiries from readers interested in landscape, pre-historic antiquities, and especially old English architecture, that the description of these backgrounds in this and its companion novels has been done from the real.'* She opened her eyes and squinted at the flapping canvas roof. 'But that's a cop-out.' She shut her eyes again and recited some more. *'In respect of places described under fictitious or ancient names—for reasons that seemed good at the time of writing—discerning persons have affirmed in print that they clearly recognize the originals; such as Shaftesbury in "Shaston" and* blah blah and he gives a long list of the real places and the fictional names and then he finishes up with *I shall not be the one to contradict them; I accept their statements as at least an indication of their real and kindly interest in the scenes.'*

She opened her eyes again gazed out at the sodden over-hanging hedgerow whistling past, turned to Tudor, and said with unexpected vehemence, 'I mean, get out of here! What sort of a cop-out is that? Give me a break. *For reasons that seemed good at the time of writing.* Like what for Chris'sake?!'

The car needed a lot of driving. The roads were tortuous and slippery. Both Tudor's hands grasped the wheel firmly, except for the manual gear changing, accomplished to the tune of flashy double-declutching.

'I suppose,' said Tudor, 'that giving real places fictitious names was liberating for him.'

'You mean he didn't have to be accurate? He could tell lies?'

'Well.' Tudor saw a single magpie out of the corner of an eye and muttered 'How's your wife?' He would have spat over his shoulder were he not concentrating so hard on keeping Daphne on the road.

Elizabeth looked at him incredulously.

'Old English custom,' he said, smiling. 'One for sorrow, two for joy. One alone is a bringer of bad luck but you break the spell if you ask him where his wife is.'

'What if the lone magpie is a Sheila not a bloke?'

'It's never a Sheila,' he said, laughing, 'single magpies are always blokes. *I am a bachelor, I live with my son. The foggy, foggy, dew.* Old Wessex ballad.'

'You're bats,' she said, 'completely bats.'

He turned left off the Cerne by-pass and

told Elizabeth that if she looked over her shoulder she would be able to see the rudest and most ancient piece of rural graffiti in Britain. Unfortunately it was too foggy to see the naked Cerne Giant with his massive erect penis. The legend was that infertile women would become pregnant if they spent the night sleeping on the giant's member.

'Appropriate symbol for Tess country, wouldn't you say?' Tudor changed down, jerkily, for the hill was steep.

'Because she was raped?'

'Yes. I bet there was a high incidence of rural rape in this part of the world. And most of it unrecorded. The county has an exceptionally feudal feel to it. Local landowners were criminally exploitative and, well, criminally rapacious. It's no coincidence that the Tolpuddle Martyrs were Wessex men. Rural employers were at least as ruthless as northern mill-owners and their ilk. But we're so conditioned by idyllic images of rural England that we won't believe it. I'd say Wessex was crawling with Alec D'Urbervilles having their way with peasant girls. How could they refuse? Without squire's patronage their families would be evicted, starve to death virtually.'

This mist was turning to fog as they ascended the hill.

'*Droit de seigneur,*' said the girl, the French words sounding odd with an Australian accent.

101

At least to an Englishman.

'Sounds better in French,' said Tudor. 'Even Strine French. It's still rape. Alec D'Urberville raped Tess in 1890 and I'd lay odds that the Tess I saw at Stonehenge yesterday has been raped at least once.'

'But under different circumstances.'

'Up to a point,' said Tudor. 'We don't have a feudal society in the old-fashioned way but we still have institutionalized, unreported rape. In nineteenth-century Wessex it was the rake-hell aristocrats and their sons who had a licence to violate any girl on the estate. Now it's . . . oh, I don't know . . . line-managers, debt-collectors, rack-rent landlords. But it still goes on: sex on demand, with menaces.'

He paused to peer through the billowing grey hill fog.

'We're here,' he said, 'Cross-in-hand. You remember in the book, Hardy says, *Of all spots on the bleached and desolate upland this was the most forlorn. It was so far removed from the charm which is sought in landscape by artists and new-lovers as to reach a kind of beauty, a negative beauty of tragic tone.*' He pulled the car over on to the greasy-green verge and stared out of the window. *'A negative beauty of tragic tone,'* he said. 'Good, eh?'

She shrugged. 'Just looks like a stone to me,' she said. She shivered. 'Bloody cold.'

'You've no soul, Elizabeth,' he said. 'That's *a strange, rude monolith from a stratum unknown in any local quarry, on which was roughly carved a human hand.* You insensitve Sheila, you. It's supposed to be the site of a murder or a miracle, possibly both. And guaranteed to *impress the most phlegmatic passer-by.'*

'Well, not this one,' she said with feeling. 'It's where D'Urberville made Tess swear never to tempt him again with her *charms and ways.* After he became a tub-thumping pretend-parson. He was on his way to preach at Abbot's Cernel or Cerne Abbas.'

'Having walked from Emminster alias Beaminster where he also preached. Not very well.'

'That is correct,' she said, like the dominatrix quiz-mistress in the TV series. 'And you're right. He didn't preach very well. Not least because he wasn't very bright. Animal cunning, maybe but no brains in any sort of academic sense.'

'Just like the real modern counterpart recently deceased,' said Tudor. 'Buckets of animal cunning but not a lot in the serious academic grey matter department. Not like us.'

The girl laughed and got out of the car, stamping her gumboots on the wet grass and pulling her Driza-bone tight about her.

'OK,' she said, 'tutorial begins. Where are we walking?'

'We're just walking,' said Tudor. 'It doesn't matter precisely where. Wessex is a cohesive landscape, all of a piece. I want us to get close to the soil, the way Hardy's characters did. And . . .' He paused, thinking, then said, 'You know, yesterday, the woman said something similar. Which is to say she accused me of not being able to begin to comprehend the world she inhabits. In Hardy you notice that the common people, the peasantry walk everywhere. They walk miles and miles on rough tracks, across uneven countryside. It must have been incredibly tough going, but it meant they were at one with nature. The aristos, though, the D'Urbervilles of the world, they travelled in sporty little dog-carts and pony-and-traps.'

'The Victorian equivalent of the sad old git's green Morgan sports car?'

'*Touché,*' said Tudor, locking the car door, and ramming his tweed cap hard down on his head. 'Let's walk.'

And so they set off along the ridge at first and then hung a right, climbed a stile and clambered down a steep muddy path into the valley. The mud was thick as treacle and mingled in occasional gateways with animal excrement to form a bog of dung-fuelled slurry. In some fields cows chewed cud morosely and gazed at them incuriously, their hoofs submerged in dark-brown muddy soil. In other fields sheep regarded them apprehensively then skittered off in a mindless, frightened flock, pausing after a while to turn and see if they were being pursued. Through the damp grey fog they could occasionally see a thatched ochre-stone farmhouse or cottage with pungent wood-smoke eddying up from the chimneys. The only sound apart from the thump and suck of their boots was the chomping of cattle and the plangent whine of the odd chain-saw.

'Where are we?' she asked, after they had been slipping and sliding for about half an hour.

Tudor shrugged. 'Somewhere in Wessex,' he said. 'Close to the earth's heartbeat. Imagine though: this is how women like Tess got from A to B. Trudge, trudge. Shanks's pony. God they must have been strong. Physically and mentally. They walked everywhere. Nowadays people gripe because of the deficiencies in the rural bus service. Bus service! Give me a break. No rural bus service in Victorian England. Not here in Wessex. If you were poor you bloody walked. And walking made you vulnerable. It made you close to the soil, it made you part of the *terroir* but it put you at risk. Fact of life. The lone pedestrian is a potential victim. Always has been, always will be. There are seldom any witnesses. When Alec D'Urberville had his wicked way with Tess out here in the countryside he knew the chances of being surprised by anyone else were infinitesimal. Likewise the chances of her reporting it.'

'You wouldn't want alfresco sex in this

105

weather,' she said, shivering. 'Not even consensual.'

'You would if you were desperate. Some of the locals even resort to sheep. And in the rain.'

She shivered again though not, this time, from the cold.

'Hello!' said Tudor suddenly. 'We have company.'

It was a Dalmatian and out apparently on its own.

'Not as remote as you thought,' she said, as the black and white dog lolloped towards them, making light work of the boggy footpath. It didn't seem remotely nervous. Rather the contrary. In fact it came right up to them, seemed to hesitate for a moment, then grabbed hold of the belt of Cornwall's riding mac and tugged at it.

'I think he's trying to tell you something,' said Elizabeth.

'She actually,' said Tudor, who prided himself on instant appraisal. The sex of animals wasn't exactly rocket science but he had always enjoyed the Sherlockian trait of being able to rattle off an instant thumbnail sketch on the flimsiest evidence. 'Ah, Watson, thirty-seven-year-old botanist with a wife in Peru and a mistress in Uxbridge.' That sort of thing.

He bent down to examine the identity tag attached to the dog's collar and read out loud,

'Lily, c/o Revd Peter Lillywhite, The Vicarage, Digby Matravers.' There was a postal code and a phone number.

'Well, Lily,' said Tudor, 'where's your master? Does he know you're out in the wilds on your own?'

As if in answer Lily relinquished her bite on his belt, stepped back and barked at him two or three times. It was not an aggressive bark, more like an attempt at canine conversation.

'She's trying to tell you something,' said Elizabeth, not very helpfully, as Lily stopped barking, grabbed hold of the belt again and tugged.

'I think she's trying to say "Come with me",' said Tudor, and followed. Seeing that he was doing as he was told Lily let go and set off in advance, turning every so often to look over her shoulder and make sure that they were following.

'Cute dog,' said Elizabeth approvingly.

They walked for just over five minutes, through woodland at first, then across a stream and into a sheep-filled field. At the far end of this there was a dry-stone wall with a stile in one corner. Lily ran ahead and stood at the stile, barked once or twice, then squeezed through a gap to one side and vanished.

Tudor and Elizabeth followed. As Elizabeth climbed over the stile, she gasped, then half-laughed, and called to her teacher.

'It's the vicar!'

107

CHAPTER TWELVE

It *was* the vicar of Digby Matravers.

He had stumbled on the stile, pitched forward into the mud and twisted his ankle. The faithful Lily had gone in search of help.

'They say Dalmatians aren't very bright,' he said to his rescuers, 'but if that's so they can't have taken Lily into account.'

Lily, for her part was licking her master's face and wagging her tail in dual expressions of relief and pride. 'What a good dog am I,' she seemed to be saying.

'Stupid thing to do,' said the Reverend Lillywhite. 'Not getting any younger. Used to be a bit of a pole-vaulter in my youth. Now defeated by common-or-garden stile on country ramble. Sign of age. Vexing, very.'

'If we support you on either side do you think you can make it home?' asked Tudor.

The vicar looked thoughtful. 'Bit of a three pipe question but, hell's bells, we should manage it all right. Not more than half a mile and downhill all the way. Would ring the wife but left the mobile in my study. Idiotic. Don't care for walkie-talkie but bit of a life-saver at times like this. Deuced lucky you were so close. Not many walkers out on a day like this. Bloody foul. Damned fine dog though.'

'Yes,' said Tudor. He hadn't thought they

made vicars like this any longer. Life was full of surprises. The reverend gentleman even sported a traditional dog-collar which was rare among modern clerics. Tudor wouldn't have been surprised to learn that he kept wicket for the Digby Matravers cricket team.

Between them Elizabeth and Tudor yanked the vicar to his feet got him to put his left arm round Tudor's shoulders and his right round Elizabeth's. Then they set off downhill very slowly and gingerly, placing their feet carefully, half dragging, half carrying the injured man while his dog walked elegantly and solicitously at their side. It was hard work but far from impossible. All three were passably fit and the vicar's uninjured leg seemed sound and supportive. After a sheep-filled field and a stretch of mixed woodland they entered a Capability Brown-type park dotted with ancient cedars and oaks with a tall-chimneyed hamstone manor house brooding in the mist on the far side of a ha-ha.

'That's "House",' said the vicar. 'Old Lady Upwey. The Upweys go back to before the Conquest but sadly the heir died of drink a few years back so when the old girl kicks the bucket the house will pass to some cousin in New Zealand. I'm told he runs a gay bar in Dunedin but you can never tell. People gossip so.'

The village started as soon as the park ended. Despite the dank, dripping day it was

109

picture-postcard pretty—all ochre stone and thatched roof. There was a smell of burning wood and the chimneys of most of the cottages exhaled a wispy, blue-grey eddy of smoke. There seemed to be bonfires around too and the whine of chain saws cut through the peace. The village stores and post office was still in business and the Blue Vinny Inn boasted the face-lift and menus of a state-of-the-stove gastro-pub. The church, the size of a small cathedral, ringed by neatly coiffed yew trees, was just beyond the Blue Vinny and the vicarage was just beyond the church. There was no sign of life anywhere and Tudor was reminded of shuttered villages in the middle of the day in north-western France. As they trudged past the church, All Saints, he noticed that the Revd Peter Lillywhite, MA (Oxon), was not only responsible for Digby Matravers but also for the neighbouring villages of Wingfield Matravers, Kenelm Matravers and Harriman Matravers. Not much time for cricket.

The vicarage was a gem. Amazing, thought Tudor, that it hadn't been sold off by the Church like so many of its old rectories and vicarages. It was built in the same yellowish hamstone as the church and every other house in the village, but it was much grander than the cottages, being slate-roofed and three-storeyed. The elegance and proportions suggested Georgian or just possibly William

110

and Mary. The windows were sashed, and the handsome front door had a heavy brass knocker, but before any of them had a chance to use it or the bell push at the side, it opened and a sensible-looking middle-aged woman in sensible shoes and a sensible twin-set was framed against the hallway.

'Oh, darling,' she said, 'what *have* you been doing? You're filthy. Absolutely covered in mud.'

'I fell,' said the vicar mildly, 'and I'd have caught my death of cold if Lily hadn't used her loaf and got help in the shape of Dr Cornwall and his friend.'

Cornwall gave a start and almost dropped his half of the crippled cleric.

'I never told you my name,' he protested, but was over-talked by the lady of the house saying, 'Hello. I'm Dorothy Lillywhite. It's very kind of you to bring him back. He's becoming simply impossible. Darling, you just can't be trusted to behave, can you? I'm so sorry. I'd normally ask you through to the drawing-room but with the state Peter's in I think you'd better bring him through into the kitchen. I'll lead the way.'

Saying which she clipped sensibly off down the hall leaving them to follow in her wake.

They followed slowly, Lily, the Dalmatian, still in close attendance, across the hall and down a dark corridor and then into a large kitchen which was as sensible as Mrs Lillywhite

111

with a large elderly cream Aga cooker, a double sink which looked original, comfortable wooden chairs some with arms, all with cushions and a smell of something stew-like cooking.

'Put him there,' said Mrs Lillywhite, not as unkindly as it sounded, and gesturing at one of the sturdier of the wooden armchairs. Tudor and Elizabeth lowered Lillywhite into it and stood looking down at him.

'I expect everyone would like a nice cup of tea,' said Mrs L, asking the question in a tone which implied that 'yes' was the only acceptable answer.

The Reverend Lillywhite looked at his watch as a certain sort of Englishman always does when he would like a snifter of alcoholic beverage but suspects that the sun is not yet over the yard-arm, and said, without much hope in his voice, 'I rather thought that given the circumstances and the perfectly bloody weather our guests might like something rather stronger.'

'For heaven's sake, Peter,' said his wife, 'It's barely half past eleven. A nice mug of Earl Grey and a digestive biscuit will do just as well.'

There was not the slightest room for argument. Lily, in a basket by the stove, looked up at them fondly but with just a suspicion of raised eyebrow.

'So how did you know who I was?' asked

Tudor.

The vicar smiled. 'I'd like to be able to say that I knew by some powerfully forensic means of deduction,' he said, 'but I have to admit that it's simply because I've been to a couple of your lectures. I was at "Red Flag to Speed Camera", your analysis of motoring offences, and also your "Bloody Assize" talk, the one where you laid into Judge Jeffreys. Both fascinating in their very different ways. Crime is something of a hobby of mine. I suspect it is for most clergymen. We see so much of it.

Tudor smiled. 'Not in a place like Digby Matravers surely,' he said, in a world-weary way.

Ah,' said Lillywhite, 'I know your work too well to believe that you fall into the trap of thinking that you associate crime and corruption entirely with the Great Wen. I believe that deviation from the socially acceptable is far more common and generally more interesting in remote and relatively self-contained places such as this than in the inner city. There is a sameness about what goes on when the population is dense. And remember what the Great Writer said—"Every village has its idiosyncrasy, its constitution, often its own code of morality." So true, so very true. Why even in the parishes to which I have the privilege of ministering, there is a quite different character to each. We have four Matraverses, as I expect you know—Digby,

113

Wingfield, Kenelm and Harriman. And each one quite unlike the other in almost every conceivable respect.'

'Including criminal?' This was Elizabeth.

'I'm afraid so,' said Lillywhite. 'Any manner of nefariousness goes on in this part of the world but there are interesting delineations. Harriman Matravers, for example, seems to have a high incidence of credit-card fraud and tax evasion. That I suppose has something to do with the socio-economic profile. The village has a large number of ABs. People commute to and from London. Kenelm Matravers, however, which is still virtually feudal with nearly everyone in a tied cottage of one kind and another, and many people still working for the estate, has a much less sophisticated criminal profile—drunkenness, disorderly behaviour, grievous bodily harm, affray, petty theft, breaking and entering. The villagers behave there much as they would have done in the eighteenth century or even earlier. They have the highest incidence of incest of any parish in the whole of Wessex. Bestiality too, or so I'm told. "The abominable crime" as the local magistrates tend to call it.'

Mrs Lillywhite came to the table with a large black teapot of steaming Earl Grey. Its bergamot fumes vied with the meat and vegetables stewing away in the Aga.

'And here?' asked Tudor. 'What about Digby Matravers?'

'Ah.' The vicar looked almost smug. 'Digby Matravers,' he said, 'is the least criminal of the four. Even the Blue Vinny is almost the exact opposite of a den of iniquity. The place is almost a temperance hall. Indeed I sometimes wish it were a little more exciting.'

'And what do you put this down to?'

'Oh, Peter thinks it's because of him,' said Mrs Lillywhite, pouring tea. She gave the impression of being the sort of wife who was in the habit of answering questions addressed to her husband. Tudor wondered how she went down in the village. Vicars' wives were more significant than most significant others. The Reverend Lillywhite seemed a rather good egg in an age when the Church of England had barely enough to make an omelette. Even the above average ones tended to be curate's eggs, he mused, realizing that his private oviferous metaphor was in danger of running away with itself. Not a good idea to put them all in one basket, not possible to make aforesaid omelette without breaking some, etcetera.

Out loud he heard himself murmuring 'Really' in a way which sounded as if he wasn't paying attention. That was clearly what Mrs Lillywhite thought for she gave him a sharp look and said, 'Yes, really.'

'It's a bit like having a village bobby, which we don't. An ambulatory priest is an active deterrent. Not that we are completely criminal-free. But even when we do have resident criminals they tend to pursue their profession beyond the parish boundaries.'

'You mean,' said Elizabeth, 'that your local villains don't foul their own nests, don't shit in their own back yard.'

This elicited another reproving look from the vicar's wife although the vicar himself didn't seem unduly disturbed.

'Something like that,' he said. 'Even when we had some quite serious professionals in the village they went away to Sandbourne or even London to do their business.'

'Serious professionals,' repeated Tudor. 'You had serious professional criminals here in Digby Matravers?'

'Rather,' said the vicar, stressing the second syllable in an old-fashioned, schoolboyish fashion. 'I'll say we did. The village didn't care for it. Major Rodney in particular. There were petitions. Anonymous letters. Not a happy episode. A house divided. I preached on their behalf. Our Lord after all—'

'Was soft on crime,' said Mrs Lillywhite. 'As were you, Peter.'

'The sin, not the sinner,' said her husband. 'I most certainly am not soft on crime any more than was Our Lord. I confess I quite liked them, indeed found them rather fascinating. And their crimes were essentially minor and nearly always non-violent.'

'The woman was nothing more than a common prostitute and one of the men was a

116

habitual conman and swindler.

'And,' said her husband, 'they had been convicted of their crimes and served their sentence. They were entitled to rehabilitation and understanding.'

'Not if they persistently re-offend.'

'Darling, we don't know that they were persistently re-offending.' The vicar looked as if he was about to dig in his heels.

'Don't be so naive,' said his wife, harshly, 'and now look what's happened!'

'What *has* happened?' The hairs on the back of Tudor's neck were prickling because he was almost certain he knew the answer.

He was right.

'The man was found stabbed to death in a B and B in Sandbourne,' she said, 'and they've arrested the little minx and charged her with murder. It's been in the papers. I should have thought you'd have known.'

CHAPTER THIRTEEN

Elizabeth Burney looked at the vicar, the vicar's wife and her supervisor and shook her head several times as if trying to get rid of some tiresome blockage in the brain.

'Whoa!' she said eventually, exhaling through her nostrils like a horse. 'That's some chain of coincidences.'

'Coincidences always come in chains,' said Tudor, 'that's why solutions to crime always fit together like jig-saws. Well'—he paused, as if shocked by the over-neat generalization—'up to a point. What we call coincidences are usually nothing of the sort.'

'Doctor Cornwall's right in a way, although as a man of the cloth I take a slightly different view of "coincidence". If you believe in God there is an element of predestination, pre-ordination, inevitability, which precludes the concept of chance altogether.'

'You mean He moves in mysterious ways?' said Elizabeth, and the vicar nodded, obviously aware that she was being facetious but not wishing to make an issue of it.

'Everything in life has a meaning,' he said, 'but unfortunately that meaning is often obscure. Obscure to us. To Almighty God it's crystal clear, but to us poor mortals many aspects of life are, as you put it, mysterious. I sometimes think of Him as the Great Detective. Without him we would simply be characters in an Agatha Christie novel living in a state of perpetual incredulity never knowing who had done anything nor why. It is God's purpose to give us the answers, to provide the solutions, solve the puzzles. The Almighty maketh all clear. If you see what I mean.'

Neither of his visitors were entirely sure they *did* see what he meant but neither admitted as much. They also wondered whether he always used three words or phrases when one would do and suspected it was a device used to add weight to an otherwise flimsy sermon.

'Can you tell us a little more about this unusual *ménage?*' asked Tudor. 'You see,' he continued, sensing a certain professional reticence on behalf of the padre and a definite narrowing of the eyes on the part of his wife, 'I do have a professional as distinct from a purely academic interest. Superintendent Trythall is an old friend of mine. Unofficially and off the record I am helping the police with their enquiries. However, for reasons I'm sure you understand they prefer not to admit it. It's a bit like the England football team bringing in a faith healer.'

'Or the cricketers appointing a chaplain,' the Reverend Lillywhite laughed. 'I always feel that when it comes to cricket Our Lord is more of an umpire than a participant,' he said, and winced suddenly. 'You know, darling, I really think that a little sherry is in order not just as a gesture of hospitality to our guests but also as a panacea for my leg which is playing up something rotten. Beyond prayer, I fear. And it must be past noon even if the sun is not yet over the yard-arm. In any case, I do think the English habit of looking at one's wrist watch whenever one is offered a drink is curiously unattractive. I do see the necessity for licensing hours, but surely not in one's own home. They don't, after all, pertain in the House of God.'

Tudor supposed he was referring to Communion wine which seemed a rather far-fetched allusion but he let it pass. Dorothy Lillywhite fixed her husband with a gorgon-like, I'll-speak-to-you-later stare but rather surprisingly rose and strode to a stripped-pine Shakerish sideboard from which she extracted four sherry glasses and, also surprisingly, a bottle of Domecq's La Ina which Tudor knew from his investigations into the death of Diana, Princess of Wales, to have been one of several favourite tipples of Her Majesty the Queen Mother. Mrs Lillywhite poured more generously than anyone expected and with a surprisingly shaky hand.

'Good health,' said the Reverend Lillywhite, taking a generous mouthful and not quite smacking his lips. 'They came, as it were from nowhere, which is where, in a sense they ultimately returned. Some people do, you know. One notices it as a vicar. In a relatively remote rural community such as this there is, for most of the population, a very considerable degree of continuity from, if you like, old Mrs Upwey in House to the most poverty-stricken and insignificant family on the estate. Indeed you could say that God's representative in country parishes are a less permanent presence than that of the natives. Priests come and priests go but most country folk go on for ever.'

He paused and looked round the little group evidently pleased with this piece of social insight, rather as if he were G.M. Trevelyan delivering himself of an aphorism.

'How long ago?' asked Tudor.

'I could look it up,' said the vicar, but as he did, his wife said crisply, 'It was the fifth Sunday after Pentecost three years ago. Early July. And they left on the fourth Sunday of Lent almost three years later. Mothering Sunday.'

'I often say,' said her husband, 'that Dorothy should have been the vicar and I should have been the wife.'

A look passed between them which did not seem to their guests to be as full of Christian love and affection as it should have been.

'So you've no idea where they had been before they came here?' said Tudor.

Once again a glance passed between them that was more hostile than one might have expected. Her expression said 'Shut up you silly old fool, let's all drink up our sherry and get these people out of the house before you say something you regret.' His said, 'I'm fed up with being nagged and patronized by you even if you do think you're a stronger, cleverer personality. For once in my life I shall say what I like and don't you dare try to stop me.'

'Yes, at first it was only the woman and the man who called himself D'Urberville,' said the vicar.

'What makes you say man who called himself D'Urberville?' asked Tudor.

The vicar shrugged. 'I'm not altogether sure,' he replied. 'I suppose he could have been called D'Urberville but it seemed inherently unlikely. There were D'Urbervilles around here but they died out long ago—even before the time Hardy wrote his novel. He struck me as a serial fantasist. I sensed he liked the sound D'Urberville made. Also that it gave him confidence, the way some men wear an Eton tie even when they've never been near the place.' He half-choked on his sherry. Lily, the Dalmatian, stretched and yawned in her basket next to the Aga. Mrs Lillywhite continued to look daggers. 'Perhaps especially men who haven't been educated at Eton. It always seems to me that if you're happy in yourself and confident in who you are you assume no airs and graces, let alone striped ties to which you are not entitled. But, no, I don't think he was a D'Urberville though it's a free country and part of me believes that a man, or a woman come to that, can call themselves whatever they like.'

'Darling, you know perfectly well that the little man called himself D'Urberville so that he could extract money from the gullible. Especially the snobbish gullible of whom I am afraid we have too many. He was a crook and name changes were part of his crookery.'

The vicar grimaced. 'My job is to hate the sin but love the sinner and besides, whatever the man, whoever he was, did, I believe it was mainly criminal rather than sinful and I believe there is a distinction.'

'Oh darling, really!' Dorothy Lillywhite looked as if she were about to throw her glass at her husband.

'And another thing,' he said, 'he never fouled his own back yard. He never even tried to pass off a dud cheque in Digby Matravers or even steal apples.'

'He was an habitual criminal,' she said, 'and she was no better. The bus was a deathtrap and insanitary. We'd won "Best Kept Village" two years running before they came. Not much hope after they'd arrived.'

'Did you know them well?' asked Tudor, directing the question at the vicar's wife.

'I should think not,' she snapped. 'I saw them from afar and I didn't like what I saw. Peter, on the other hand, visited the bus on a regular basis which I'm afraid some of his congregation found intolerable. They were certainly smoking cannabis on the premises. Maybe worse.'

'I keep saying,' protested the Reverend Lillywhite, 'that they were as much sinned against as sinning. In a strange sort of way I rather liked him. Her too. I certainly preferred them to some of the prigs who've moved into the village in recent years.'

And here again he glared at his wife who glared back.

'Besides, it ill behoves us to speak ill of the dead. Whatever he was I don't feel he deserved a violent death in a squalid boarding-house in Sandbourne.'

'It wasn't particularly squalid,' said Tudor. 'What was it like in the bus?'

The vicar hesitated. 'Not what you or I are used to,' he said. 'The dog didn't help. A badly bred Alsatian. I'm always surprised by the way impoverished travellers always seem to have dogs that must cost a fortune to feed. The smell was ghastly I have to admit. Dog, human BO, stale cigarettes, cooking fat, beer. But that was their problem. No one had to go in there. They weren't exactly gregarious. Kept themselves to themselves.'

'*You* had to go in there,' said Elizabeth.

'Up to a point,' he conceded, 'I felt it was my duty to do so. Others wouldn't.'

'What about the police,' asked Tudor. 'Social services? All that sort of thing. After all we seem to have government inspectors to regulate every conceivable aspect of human behaviour. The authorities must have been after them.'

'Indeed,' said Lillywhite whose wife had fallen uncharacteristically silent and poured herself another glass of La Ina without offering any to the other three, 'I felt they were being hassled. Whatever harm they might

124

have been doing each other they were doing none to us and none to our immediate community. If, when they ventured further afield, they offended the law then it was the job of the law so to behave appropriately but it was not for us. I was not proud of what happened here.'

'What exactly did happen?' asked Elizabeth.

'If,' said the vicar, 'we were in a western you'd have to say they were run out of town. The local children taunted them whenever they went out and sometimes threw stones at the bus. Their parents wouldn't intervene. The village shop wouldn't serve them. Nor the Blue Vinny.'

Mrs Lillywhite could evidently stand it no longer.

'Darling,' she said, in not very good control of her voice which sounded high-pitched and strangulated, 'how can you? If the shop or the pub had served them their business would have gone right down the drain. All their regulars would have gone off to Harriman or Wingfield. They'd have driven them out. The smell apart from anything else. And the foul language.'

'Oh come, Dorothy,' he said, 'neither was as bad as you make out. Both a bit ripe for the average taste I concede, but not seriously offensive.

'It all sounds rather sad to me,' said Tudor, meaning it. 'Did you talk much?'

'The man was far from unintelligent. Well read too, though basically an autodidact with all the defensive arrogance that the word implies. I certainly enjoyed conversation with him. We talked often about crime and about Thomas Hardy. He was well informed about both and if his ideas were hare-brained at least he had ideas.'

'You haven't mentioned the third party,' said Elizabeth suspiciously. 'The Hell's Angel from County Clare. He was with the woman when they arrested her at Stonehenge. Tudor was there.'

'Ah.' The vicar and his wife stared at each other, daggers now clearly drawn, but for a long time neither said a word. Eventually Peter Lillywhite broke the silence.

'I'm afraid the third party is something of a sore point. I suppose in the end, er, I, that is Dorothy and I,' he wrung his hands in some distress. 'I'm not quite sure how to put this.'

'Oh, darling,' said Dorothy Lillywhite, sounding exasperated but suddenly and unexpectedly fond, 'there's no point in pretending.' She turned to Tudor and for a moment he thought she was going to break down and weep.

'You see, Dr Cornwall,' she said, 'the Hell's Angel from County Clare, as you describe him, is our son Robert.'

126

CHAPTER FOURTEEN

The class had a mulish feel to it the day after the curious encounter at Digby Matravers. Tudor was intrigued by group dynamics, crowd behaviour, the mob, mass hysteria and the stuff one of his favourite historians, George Rude, was always writing about. You could hardly call his little class a crowd but there was an animal, visceral quality to their mood. This morning it was as if they had a collective hangover. They seemed uniformly surly, sullenly silent. Tudor could not put his finger on the reason even though he felt he had a finger on the pulse. The weather was dark and dank; the national news dismal and the Education Secretary was proposing huge top-up fees. You couldn't blame the class for being ill-tempered.

'I'm going to read you a very short passage from my *Tess* rewrite,' he said.

The response to this was nothing as audible as a group groan but he sensed a tangible sigh of uninterest. They looked positively narcoleptic. He didn't *feel* boring but then, he supposed, bores never did. He cleared his throat and began to read.

The dark brown thud of the closing main gate of the prison behind them always

127

induced a feeling somewhere between panic and depression in both 'Ranter Reuben and his trusty servant, Ledlow. The closing of the door to Wintoncester Gaol was no exception and although their incarceration was entirely voluntary neither man felt comfortable. The uniformed warder with the jangling keys at his belt was perfectly friendly and the governor, through whose good offices this visit had been arranged, had been Reuben's company sergeant major when their regiment, Rodney's Horse, had been stationed on the North West Frontier.

True to their former relationship the governor snapped to attention as Reuben and Ledlow were ushered into his office, which was sparsely furnished and decorated only with a large sepia print of Queen Victoria. Reuben bit back a desire to say, as he used to, 'At ease Perkins,' but instead, said simply, 'Very good to see you, Harry.' Then indicating his companion he added, 'You remember Ledlow. Used to be my batman.'

'Indeed yes. Very good to see you too Ledlow.'

They all sat.

'You'll find the prisoner in a very subdued frame of mind, I'm afraid,' said the governor. 'Barely speaks, eats hardly at all. Even the chaplain who's a first-rate chap is

finding her difficult. He says she seems to have given up the will to live.'

'I'm sorry to hear it,' said Reuben. 'I dare say the sooner I talk to her the better.'

Here Tudor broke off, sensing an increase in the class's lack of attention.

'Right,' he said, 'we're all set up and ready to go. We know that Reuben is a great detective in Holmesian mode and we know that Tess is pleading guilty and seems to have given up on everything and everybody. So the three of them will go down to the cells where Tess will be in solitary. The guv will show in Reuben—and Ledlow as well, I suppose, though we might have second thoughts about that. Then what's going to happen? It's Reuben's shout, his initiative but the woman doesn't know him from a bar of soap. They've never met. So how does he start?'

'He has to win her confidence.' This was from Freddie, expressed with a very male certainty.

'That's not possible.' This was Tamsin, disagreeing with equal certainty, female and Celtic. 'Every man in her life has betrayed her: her father is a negligent drunk; Alec makes her pregnant; Angel marries her and then abandons her when she confesses the truth about her illegitimate child; then Alec reappears and marries her, treating her disgustingly and taunting her when weedy

129

Angel comes back from South America and says he still loves her. And Alec has said that Angel will never reappear so that's another betrayal. I mean all right so it's heaped on, but everything in her life has taught her that men can't be trusted. And now this fancy-hat from London comes mincing into her cell with his gentleman's gentleman and the governor and asks her to trust him. I mean per-lease.'

She stopped, flushed, realizing that she had spoken with a passion not appropriate to an academic discussion in the twenty-first century. It would have gone down a treat in the 1890s and, perhaps, with Tess herself. Modern times demanded something more dessicated and forensic.

'Sorry,' she said.

'No need,' said Tudor. 'Good that one of you actually cares about the issues involved.'

He looked round the room. 'So,' he said, 'which one is right?'

'We're not disagreeing,' said Freddie, very slowly. 'I think we think the guy's got to win her confidence but we think he's got a tough call. Tamsin's right, she's not there to have her confidence won. It's damaged beyond repair. Especially where men are concerned.'

'Do you think she did it?' asked Tudor, and was met with much shuffling and staring at the ground. Nobody seemed to know. Maybe nobody cared though he wasn't sure about that.

'The only real question,' said Karl, the punk vegetarian pacifist, 'is did you do it?' We have to assume that the police have asked her this already and she's said yes and that's all there is to it.'

'Except,' said Tamsin, 'that she's given up. She's resigned to her fate. Even if she said she wasn't guilty she doesn't think anyone else would believe her, least of all a male judge and jury. So whether she did or whether she didn't, the easiest thing is to put her hands up and say it's a fair cop and I'm guilty as hell and get the whole thing over with. She wants to die. It's obvious and it's simple. Well, straightforward. That's why Hardy doesn't faff around with interrogations and court-room scenes.'

'But Conan Doyle would?' Tudor asked.

'But Conan Doyle would have been wasting his time,' said Freddie, implying insolently, that Tudor was doing the same thing. And wasting theirs as well.

'But,' Tudor persisted, 'if she was innocent then we, society if you like, have a duty to make sure that justice prevails.'

'Even,' asked Frances, 'if that goes against her wishes? She wants death not justice. Can't she be allowed at least one thing she wants? She's never been allowed anything else.'

'That's what seems to have happened in the authorized version,' said Tudor. 'She just gave up, pleaded guilty, had the plea accepted and was duly strung up. End of sad story. But if she *wasn't* actually guilty it's an even sadder story. And maybe she was covering up for someone else—for her first husband, Angel Clare, whom she still loved. And also, because she was that sort of person, the thought that by removing herself from life she would leave the way open for her little sister Liza-Lu to marry Angel and live happily ever after.'

'That's sick,' said Frances.

'I'm inclined to agree,' said Tudor, 'but we're getting away from the question of what Reuben should do to win Tess's confidence—even if you do all think it's impossible. If he comes over all sentimental and over-friendly she won't trust him. She's seen it all too often before. If he's blunt and to the point and asks what we assume the police and her defence counsel—if she has such a thing which I doubt—have already done on countless occasions she'll clam up even more. So tell me: what would Sherlock Holmes have done? Or Peter Wimsey? Or even Hercule Poirot?'

There was more shuffling and avoidance of eye contact.

He hated this. Only a handful of members of the class ever contributed and when they failed to speak the basis of the way he taught was completely destroyed. He knew colleagues who droned uninterrupted through class after class while those who sat at their feet took note after note and then at the appropriate moment regurgitated them by rote in answer to predictable questions in predictable exams and end of semester essays. That way lay tedium and mediocrity.

'Little grey cells,' he ventured, 'that's what distinguishes the great detective from the lumpen proletariat, isn't it? What distinguishes Holmes from Watson is not Watson's dogged stupidity but Holmes's brilliance. The great detective always seems to know more than anyone else and it doesn't really matter whether his superior knowledge and insights derive from forensic leaps and bounds, an exhaustive and incisive examination of all the available evidence or simply inside information. It has been said that the top-flight journalist is only as good as his telephone or contacts book. The same is true of the great detective of the golden age and before. Men like Holmes, Wimsey and Campion are almost impossibly well-connected in an age when good connections were synonymous with high society. Campion was supposed to be a royal from the wrong side of the blanket; Wimsey's was a ducal family, quite apart from the fact that he was a Balliol man: Holmes was a more mysterious figure but clearly, in a word, well-connected. Some critics think they were created in this way because their authors were snobbish but I don't believe this is so. They lived at a time and in a society which was dominated by a small group of grandees and part of their apparent omniscience derives from the fact that they are an integral part of that closed society.

'That's slightly beside the point, but the point I'm making is germane. Reuben can't win Tess over by sympathy or kindness but he might stun her by his cleverness or by his inside knowledge. The people who have questioned her so far don't know her secrets. Indeed they know virtually nothing about her. And that gives her the strength to withstand their questioning.'

Tudor glared round the class looking for signs of comprehension or even interest. He received very little by return and swore inwardly.

'Very well', he said, 'let me demonstrate by reading Tranter Reuben's first question to the accused.' He paused for theatrical effect and then read, *'Tell me, my dear, how it was that you came to kill the horse?'*

He stared around the class again and was rewarded with barely a flicker of anything. He wondered how many of them had actually read the original *Tess*. If they had they didn't show much sign of remembering it.

There was a long silence.

'Very well,' he said, at length, 'I want you to write an essay for next week on whether or not Tess was responsible for the death of Prince, whether this death ruined her father's job as a haggler, whether she really dragged her family into a quagmire, whether her mother's solution to the disaster had an ulterior motive, and what was the significance of the fact that Alec D'Urberville's father's name was Simon Stoke. You might also care to consider whether the physical appearance of Alec and Tess in any way determine their character and what relevance this has to their ultimate fate. Oh, and I should like at least a paragraph on whether or not Simon Stoke was a money-lender from up north and if so whether this fact has any significance.'

'That's an awful lot of questions.' protested Freddie.

'That, dear boy,' said Tudor, with exasperation, 'is how crime is solved. By the asking of questions. And an awful lot of them. I'll see you next week,' he said, and swept angrily from the room.

As he took the steps outside two at a time he found himself wondering about some of these questions himself. He had considered them before, of course, but this new, up-to-the-minute, real-life murder gave them a different slant. The question of identity, for example. The Alec D'Urberville in Hardy's novel was no more D'Urberville than poor Al or Albert Smith who had died the previous week.

At the bottom of the stairs he closed his eyes and conjured up the relevant passage from his capacious and photographic memory.

What was it old Stoke had done? Settled in the south 'out of hail of his business district'. So he'd decided to start afresh with a name that nobody would associate with his past and 'that would be less commonplace than the original bald stark words'.

Tudor smiled and recited out loud, *'Conning for an hour in the British Museum, the pages of works devoted to extinct, half-extinct, obscured and ruined families appertaining to the quarter of England in which he proposed to settle, he considered that D'Urberville looked and sounded as well as any of them: and D'Urberville accordingly was annexed to his own name for himself and his heirs eternally.'*

He smiled to himself and repeated, louder, *'And D'Urberville accordingly was annexed to his own name for himself . . .'*

'Penny for them,' said a twangy Australian voice at his elbow, and looking down he saw Elizabeth Burney. He was immediately reminded of another passage in the original book:

For all her bouncing handsome womanliness, you could sometimes see her twelfth year in her cheeks, or her ninth sparkling from her eyes, and even her fifth would flit over the curves of her mouth now and then.

She certainly had a bouncing womanliness

136

and a wisdom beyond her years and yet sometimes she seemed far younger than she really was.

'Go on,' she said, 'penny for them.'

'Oh,' he said, 'I was pondering the question of age and identity, of how impossible it is to resist the first and how easy to change the latter. Then and now.'

And frowning, as she frowned with him, he said, also out loud, 'I wonder if he ever thought of calling himself "Smith-D'Urberville".'

CHAPTER FIFTEEN

It was several days since Tudor had given Elizabeth Burney the dead man's book and from the moment that she entered his office it was clear that this tutorial was going to be occupied by nothing else.

'Wow!' she said, sitting down on the sofa, curling her legs up and shaking her hair in enthusiastic disbelief. 'Some text. What a screwball! I mean, Jeez!'

Tudor's day had been difficult: too many classes with the dim and lethargic first years. Most of them were either hung-over or exhausted from the part-time jobs necessary to finance their studies. Too many were doing Criminal Studies because they thought it

137

offered a soft and mildly sexy option. It had been hard going and the session with little Miss Burney was the last of the working day. He liked it like that because it meant that they could end up over just the one at Henchards. He enjoyed that more than he probably should have done.

Nevertheless her exuberance irritated him.

'Calm down,' he said, 'speak more slowly. And try to talk coherently.'

She grinned at him.

'Don't tell me,' she said. 'First years have been giving you a hard time. If only the vice-chancellor knew what you have to put up with. You've been offered a professorship at Princeton. You could spend all your time doing telly. They're bloody lucky to have you. You're not appreciated.'

He relaxed, but not completely. It was disconcerting to be such an open book to someone he was supposed to be teaching.

'Tell me your findings. Do it simply and rationally. You're not a first year, remember, you're supposed to be doing a PhD.'

'OK,' she said, 'but it's sort of difficult to know where to begin. I mean, look at this.' She flicked through the pages, found what she was looking for. 'Page 96, Chapter 11, line 13. See he's underlined it again and again in red. He's done so much underlining he's almost gone through the page.'

Tudor took the book from her and frowned

over the phrase that had evidently so agitated Albert Smith, or whoever he was.

It read, *'Tess, why do you always dislike my kissing you?'*

He read it through a couple of times and looked up.

'So,' he said, 'what does this say to you?'

'Isn't it obvious?'

'To you perhaps. Maybe not to me. Anyway, tell me your interpretation.'

She made a grumpy gesture of exasperation as if to say 'Oh *men!*' Or possibly, and even more irritatingly, 'Oh, *old men!*'

'He's identifying with Alec in the book. Alec in the book desires Tess but even if he manages to kiss her he knows she hates it. He turns her off. It upsets him.'

'Who?' asked Tudor. 'Alec in the book or Alec in real life?'

'Both,' she said, with a sub-text which said 'idiot'. 'And look, on the next page, when Hardy says *'He knew that anything was better than frigidity.'* The underlinings are almost more savage than earlier. And there are seven ticks. I think they were added at different periods. The ink's a slightly different colour.'

'Do you think Hardy meant the same by "frigidity" as we do now?'

'Nice point,' she said. 'I don't think the average reader in 1890 would understand "frigidity" to mean what we now think. It has a very specific sexual meaning these days but it wouldn't then. The Victorians didn't have a technical language for sex. Did they?'

'Well, did they?' he asked quizzically.

She blushed, not because she was embarrassed to be talking about the precise sexual meaning of the word frigidity but because she didn't like admitting ignorance. Still, she was honest enough to do so when the situation demanded, as at this moment it did.

'I don't think so.'

'Freud didn't publish his *Interpretation of Dreams* till ten years after *Tess*,' said Tudor. 'But as far as Hardy's concerned that's probably insignificant. My sense is that Hardy had a considerable understanding of sex based on his own experience and also on his own intuitive perceptions. He writes well about the tensions between men and women, don't you think?'

'I do,' said Elizabeth, 'and I think our corpse recognized that. He empathized with what Hardy was saying. I also think he's interpreting the word frigidity in a modern, not a Victorian sense. He feels rejected because his Tess or Tesses don't do orgasms, don't even like sex, leastways not with him.'

'Hmm,' said Cornwall.

'Oh, listen.' said Elizabeth. 'It's sort of sweet. Page 173. '*Angel Clare had the honour of all the dairymaids in his keeping*'. Isn't that charming?'

'Up to a point,' said Tudor. 'Depends

140

exactly what you mean by "honour".'

Elizabeth gave him a piercing look.

'Your dead man asked the same question. Or rather he came up with an answer. He's done an equation mark in red and written in "virginity" with a couple of screamers.'

Tudor smiled that supercilious teacher's smile which so infuriated pupils and others.

'All you're doing is imposing modern interpretations on old-fashioned statements,' he said. 'The Victorians did euphemism, we don't. We call spades spades. They called them, oh, I don't know, soup spoons . . . whatever.'

'Don't patronize me,' said Elizabeth. 'The art of reading old books lies in cracking the code. I understand that. I wouldn't be here otherwise.'

Tudor felt only marginally put down. He enjoyed this sort of adversarial discourse. True teaching was founded on argument, answers only emerged from debate, consensus was crap.

'So have you cracked the code?'

It was Elizabeth's turn to offer a supercilious smile.

'I think so, yes.'

'Are you going to let me in on the secret?'

'Might,' she said, 'Might not.'

Long pause. Mexican stand-off.

Eventually Tudor broke the silence.

'Are you telling me you want this to be an

extra-mural activity?'

She appeared to think for a moment, then flashed him a disturbingly come-hither smile and said, 'Guess so.'

'Bottle of red at Henchards?'

She looked at her watch in the way the English did whenever anyone suggested a drink, a habit she had acquired only in the time she had spent at Wessex U.

'Rymill or Rockford?' he asked. Even when it came to a bottle of wine he had to approach the matter as if it was an academic argument. Rymill or Rockford: discuss. No more than 1500 words. Candidates should write on one side of the paper only. Academia had conditioned him to a point at which he had difficulty functioning as a recognizable human being. He couldn't switch off.

Elizabeth wasn't—yet, at least—like that. She was still a blankish sheet of paper waiting to be written on.

Henchards was almost deserted when they arrived and Tudor, in a sudden mood of oenological rebellion ordered a bottle of Rioja from Vina Alta and a packet of chilli-flavoured Doritos. Elizabeth said nothing but made an obvious mental note. In some ways she was older than he was but then, as she reflected, most women were older than most men—Tess being, in a manner of speaking, a case in point. Men were such babies she thought to herself, helping herself to a Dorito and taking a sip of the Spanish wine which, she had to admit, was almost as good as an Aussie red.

'So,' said Tudor, puckering his lips, 'shoot.'

'Well,' she said, 'he was an obvious basket-case. Completely fascist when it came to sex and women; utterly fascinated by concepts of right and wrong, property, theft, violence, murder and every aspect of crime and criminality and, of course, totally obsessed by the book. He was like a saint with the Bible or an imam with the Koran. Way beyond normality. He was a professional crook but he was miles beyond what that implies. He was a sort of professor of crookery. He didn't just practise—he preached. No, that's not right. But you know what I mean. He believed in what he did.'

'What exactly are you trying to say?' asked Tudor.

'I'm not sure.' She seemed genuinely pensive and uncertain. 'Perhaps what I'm beginning to believe is that if this bloke, whoever he was, had not been ripped untimely from his studies at Osmington then he might have been quite good academically. Might even have gone to university. Good old Wessex U even. And if he had done university what would have been his subject?'

'You're going to tell me anyway so I shan't dignify you with an answer,' said Tudor.

'Obvious I'd say.' She had an air of tentative triumph. 'He'd have gone for criminal studies.

Would probably have been a star pupil. He obviously understood the criminal mind from the inside. That's what he had: a criminal mind. He was a practitioner and a theorist too.'

'Unusual combination,' conceded Tudor, 'but it's all speculative stuff and it doesn't get as any closer to solving the mystery.' He was aware that he was sounding as prosaically pragmatic as Eddie Trythall.

A sudden squall of hail rattled against the wine-bar windows and they both shivered. British winters were particularly hellish if you had been born and brought up in Tasmania.

'OK,' she conceded, 'there's easily enough in there for a doctoral thesis, but there's also a very simple colour code I'm surprised you didn't crack. Surprised and rather shocked.'

She smirked.

'Go on,' he said, irritated.

'All the scribbles and hieroglyphics and underlinings and circlings are in different colours, right?'

'Yes,' he said, even more irritably.

'So what do you make of that?'

'Not a lot,' said Tudor. 'I assume he used whatever pen or pencil came to hand. So the colours are random.'

'I don't agree,' she said. 'Did you notice how comparatively few of the marks were in green?'

'Not especially,' he said. 'As I said, I didn't

attach much significance to the colours.'

'Well,' said the girl, 'I haven't done a detailed count but I'd say that the number of green entries is disproportionately low.'

'I don't see what you're getting at,' he said.

'Well,' she said, 'because there were so few green marks it was easy to examine them. Want to know what I found?'

'You're obviously going to tell me, so OK, yes, go ahead.'

'Right,' she said. 'The first mark is on page four, the title verso, immediately opposite the short biographical note. There's an italic line at the bottom which says that the book was printed and bound in Great Britain by Hartnolls Limited of Bodmin, Cornwall. The word he's circled, in green, is Cornwall.'

'So?' Tudor shook his head and glanced gloomily at the window panes. The hail had turned to rain but was still lashing the glass as if intent on smashing it and invading the relatively snug bar/brasserie.

'The next green entry,' she said, 'is on page 28 where Parson Tringham, the antiquary, is telling tipsy old John Durbeyfield that he's a lineal descendant of the D'Urberville who came over with William the Conqueror in 1066. You remember he then bangs on in a school-primer way talking about various Sir Johns through history. And alongside our man has written "Norman, Plantaganet, Stuart but no Tudor". And guess what?'

'Don't tell me,' said Cornwall, 'he's written it in green.'

'Good,' Elizabeth drank deeply from her glass of Rioja and crammed a Dorito into her mouth.

'Which means?'

'I should have thought that was obvious,' she said through crumbs, 'he's sending you a message from beyond the grave.'

'Don't be so melodramatic,' he said. 'That's ridiculous. People don't do things like that.'

'Most people may not,' she said, 'but we're dealing with a serious fruitcake—a man who's taken the name of a character in a Victorian novel and tried to make his life and death match up to the fiction Thomas Hardy created. So I don't think it's melodramatic to suggest he might be using the book to send you a posthumous message.'

Tudor sighed. 'So what's the message?'

'Well,' she said, 'it's not exactly long or complicated. There isn't another bit of green until page 248. He's ringed the number and then at the bottom of the first paragraph there's a reference to the King's Arms, Casterbridge, where the venerable postilion worked. He's ringed "King's". Then the next entry comes just four pages later at the beginning of chapter 34 which starts *They drive by the level road along the valley . . . .*". He's drawn a green circle round "road".' She paused. 'Are you getting the hang of it?'

He nodded. 'Two-hundred-and-forty-eight King's Road. Are you serious about this?'

'Well, why not?' she wanted to know. 'It makes sense so far, doesn't it?'

'Go on then,' he said, 'you've obviously got a conclusion.'

'Page 444,' she said, 'the next two splodges of green. Three lines up from the end of Chapter 58 and there's green round the capital "S" of "She". Then in the very first line of the next chapter he's put green round the "W" of "Wintoncester". And, finally, when you get to the bibliography he's put a green ring around the last two digits of the year of publication of *Satires of Circumstance.*'

'*Lyrics and Reveries,*' said Tudor, thankful for a chance to demonstrate that he was neither completely ignorant nor totally thick. '1914 unless I'm much mistaken. So if you're right then he's telling me to look for something at 248 King's Road, SW14. That's East Sheen from memory. Between Putney and Richmond.'

'So what do you think?' she asked, leaning back on her heavy wooden wagon-wheel chair and smiling at her teacher with the look of someone who expects at least an alpha plus.

'I think you're a clever girl,' he said patronizingly, adding, in an unworthy attempt to regain the advantage, 'and one who's been exceedingly well taught!'

147

CHAPTER SIXTEEN

The woman was looking much improved. This was not difficult for on that dismal morning in the Stonehenge car-park she had resembled a rag doll. Tudor found it difficult to give her a personality or even an identity. In fact he was having trouble with 'identity' which was becoming an ever more illusory concept for him. He hated thinking of her as Tess. Much less D'Urberville. 'Al's moll' was his preferred moniker but he could see that this was facetious.

The remand centre to which she had been consigned was a brand new, custom-built 'facility', built with European funding as part of a pilot scheme dreamed up by an expensive government committee of progressive thinkers. It was for women only and the regime was determinedly enlightened and humane. Al's moll was far better off here than she had been in the decrepit bus. She was scrubbed up and wearing regulation blue overalls that looked like a cross between dungarees and a boiler suit and she looked almost happy.

They sat in the corner of a comfortable, chintzy lounge which felt more like a family hotel than a holding camp for unconvicted murderesses. They even had poor reproduction of *Salisbury Cathedral* by Constable, *Sunflowers* by Van Gogh with *Country Life* and *Hello!* magazines on the coffee tables.

'So,' said Tudor genially, 'this is better than the Sultan's Harem I should think.'

The sunny beam changed swiftly to a frosty glare but switched back fast.

'You've been talking to your mate Trythall,' she said.

'Yes,' he said, evenly, 'and he and his colleagues have put together most of the story.'

'But not the whole jigsaw.'

'No,' he agreed, 'not the whole jigsaw.'

They stared at each other, unblinking, like two poker players. Or maybe chess.

Eventually the woman spoke. 'I'm not saying more than I killed Al and I'm pleading guilty. That's it.'

'I know that's what you're saying,' said Tudor, 'and I know that's how you're pleading. That's not what I'm interested in.'

They engaged in another stare, daring one another to draw the next card, or risk a pawn.

She led first.

'So what exactly are you interested in?'

'You,' he said. Which was true, but also trumped her line.

'OK,' she said, tossing her head. Even her hair seemed to have regained some natural lustre and bounce. 'Shoot.'

'Tell me about the Sultan's Harem.'

She shrugged. 'Not a lot to say. Clean. All girl. No exploitation. Friendly atmosphere. Reasonable rates. Nice class of punter.'

'How did you find it?'

'I dunno. Yellow Pages. Personal recommendation. It's so long ago. It was a nice place to work. I hope you don't tell your friend Trythall any lies about it because we never had any trouble. Not once. In fact some of the local police were good customers. I think they should legalize them.'

'What, massage parlours?'

'Oh sod passage parlours: it's a brothel. Nothing more, nothing less. The guys pay their money and the girls give them what they pay for. There's loads of mutual respect. And if someone wants to pay a hundred quid to dress up in women's clothes or have me spank his bum wearing a black leather leotard, well what harm's it doing anyone?'

'Selling your body's not most people's idea of a nice thing to do.'

'That's a very pompous remark. Particularly from a Reader in Criminal Studies. Al would have been disappointed in you.'

'What did Al say about me?'

'That's for you to find out.'

'Did Al predict my wanting to talk to you?'

She gave this some thought and then said, 'Yes. Al gave me very specific instructions about what I was to say to you. And what I wasn't allowed to talk about. And I'll do as he told me.'

'So he knew about me?'

She thought again.

'Yes, he knew about you, but that's all I'm saying about him and you.'

'How did you two meet?'

'In a pub.'

'What pub?'

'The Blue Vinny in Digby Matravers.'

'But you only moved to Digby Matravers three years ago.'

'I'm a Wessex girl,' she said, 'and Al's a Wessex lad. Or was. Not many places in Wessex we don't know. I was working behind the bar for a few weeks an age ago. I'd only just left school. Al was selling cigarettes. He came in one night and ordered a pint of mild. And that was it.'

'Love at first sight?'

She giggled 'Something like that. Maybe not love exactly whatever that is. But something. Al could be very persuasive. The bastard.'

'So why did you kill him?'

'Pass.'

Tudor formed the impression she was enjoying this.

'He was an habitual criminal?'

'Is that a statement or a question?'

'Question.'

'Depends what you mean by criminal. Like love. I guess we both probably mean different

151

things. That's what Al always said.'

'How long had you been with him?'

'About fifteen years. Give or take.'

'And how did you live? What did you do for money?'

'Oh come on,' she said, and pulled a packet of cheap cigarettes from the breast pocket of her overalls. She lit one and exhaled through her nostrils. Smoking was forbidden in the lounge but no one seemed to care. Enforcement of the ban might be politically correct but it would also constitute an infringement of personal liberty. The women in this place might be detained at Her Majesty's pleasure and against their will but they hadn't been found guilty of anything. Not yet. No matter whether they entered a plea of innocent or guilty.

'Why do you ask?' she said. 'You must have got the picture from your friend Trythall.'

'Maybe, maybe not,' he said. 'I'd like to hear it from you.'

'The social security people were usually surprisingly generous, but then Al was bloody good at filling the forms in. Then there were all his scams. I liked the second-hand Rollers with the posh owners best.'

'I heard about that,' said Tudor. 'Very smart.'

'Couldn't see the harm in it,' she said. 'Served the buggers right. And there wasn't much wrong with the cars. Al never hurt anyone, at least not on purpose. He used to say he was in the "wealth redistribution business". He was no more a criminal than the big banks or the credit-card companies or loads of company directors and stuff. We all worked hard and we never made a lot. You've seen the bus. That's why, like I say, I'm better off here.'

Tudor didn't entirely disagree. One aspect of his work was a fascination with the criminal that occasionally drifted over into affection. It happened. He knew one distinguished prison governor who went so far as to say, in private, that he much preferred the company of murderers to that of so-called ordinary people. He wouldn't go as far as that but he had to admit that, in his experience, many villains were more entertaining than the honest John or Joanna.

The woman was, he supposed, a criminal of sorts but only in a muted, slightly desperate way. She was more of a loser than a menace.

'What about your family background?'

She laughed. 'Al said you'd ask about my family. Said you'd be really happy if you discovered I'd been abused by my dad. Sorry, no. My dad was a nice old thing. Died when I was twelve.'

'What did he do?'

'Farm labourer. Mum was in service for a while. Took in washing. There were six of us. I was the eldest.'

'You don't have a younger sister called Liza-Lu?'

She looked at him oddly. 'No,' she said, 'but Al used to call Sharon Liza-Lu. Said it suited her the same way Tess suited me. It all came from his book. He got Robbie at it as well.'

'Have you read it?'

She looked derisive 'The book? Me, no. Not a reader me. Al used to tell me about it and quote bits and pieces or read things. I didn't like it. Depressing. Life's sick enough already without muck like that but Al used to vanish into it. Weird.'

'And Robert Lillywhite?'

He had the satisfaction of seeing her look startled. She hadn't expected him to know who Robbie was and he watched her bite back the urge to ask how he had acquired this piece of information.

'What about him?'

'How did you meet?'

A long silence while she seemed to be debating whether to discuss the man. Then she said, 'At the Sultan's Harem.'

'He was a client?'

'A punter, yes.'

'Strange for a vicar's son?'

'He *is* strange for a vicar's son,' she said. 'You know what they say about convent girls. Robbie's a walking revolt against his sanctimonious parents, their middle-class values. He dropped out, went to Ireland, became a Hell's Angel. I was stupid. Talked too much. It seemed such a strange chance, his dad being the local vicar, and all that. And one day he came looking for the bus. I was shit-scared because I thought Al would take it out on me. We had a strict rule about not bringing work home from the office, but Al seemed to take a shine to Robbie right from the off. He just loved the Hell's Angels jacket from the County Clare chapter. I can see him now, the first time he saw it. Laughing like a maniac and repeating "It's meant. It's written in the book. Good old Tom" over and over again. 'Good old Tom.'

The woman lit another cigarette and stared at the ceiling. She looked as if she was playing the scene over in her head.

'So Robbie moved in?'

'Yeah, Robbie moved in.'

'What did his parents think?'

'They didn't like it. His mother especially. Mind you, the only reason she didn't like it was because of what the neighbours were saying. Silly cow! She's a snob. Robbie's dad's all right. Silly old fool but all right. I was quite fond of him in a strange way. And he didn't care tuppence about the neighbours. He was just unhappy because he felt Robbie had fallen off the path of righteousness or whatever he called it. He didn't like Robbie doing drugs and screwing around. He wanted a son who was respectable and God-fearing same as like he was. Know what I mean?'

Tudor nodded. He knew what she meant and he found himself feeling oddly depressed. He knew how the old man must have felt. Three lives wasted and one of them his own son's. Tudor, who had never knowingly fathered a child, still had it in him to empathize.

'Where's your girlfriend?'

The question took him by surprise.

'Sorry,' he said, 'girlfriend what girlfriend?'

'She was with you the other day. At Stonehenge. Pretty little Australian. Young enough to be your daughter.'

'She's not a girlfriend, she's a PhD. student. Very bright.'

'How was she chosen?'

'Well,' he said, 'it's a long story.'

This was true.

'Must be difficult choosing your students. Must be hundreds of applicants with identical qualifications. Strange you should go for such an attractive young girl. You wouldn't have chosen a bloke you weren't attracted to.'

'It doesn't work like that,' he said, 'the procedures for admission to the university are incredibly rigorous. If I were to admit students simply because I fancied them I'd be slung out. Rightly so.'

'Huh,' she said, 'believe that and you'll believe anything.'

Once more they stared at each other. There

was a mutual incomprehension there, but also, Tudor sensed, a mutual curiosity.

'If you did it,' he said, eventually, 'if you killed Al, why did you do it?'

She gazed back at him.

'I said I wasn't going to discuss the murder,' she said.

'I know.'

'But now you're asking me to tell you whether I had a motive.'

'Yes.'

'Bloody cheek!'

'Maybe.'

'Tell me something,' she said, 'you're head of a department which spends all its time studying people like me and Al and Robbie. And you think you understand what makes us tick. And part of what you believe is that what you call crimes always have to have motives. You think everything has to have a reason. You want everything to have an explanation; you want it all to make sense. But me and Al and Robbie don't always see it like that. We think that's not always true. I may not have had what you call a reason for killing Al. You don't have a reason for everything you do. You eat strawberries because you like strawberries; you drink champagne because you enjoy it. Why not the same with crime? Or murder even? Like the man said about Mount Everest, it's there.'

Must murder have motive? Tudor thought

to himself. Discuss.

Thinking which, he said a not altogether convincing goodbye to Al's self-confessed killer, made his excuse and left.

For all sorts of reasons, he decided, she was better off inside.

CHAPTER SEVENTEEN

'*Tess looked, to Tranter Reuben, like a woman already dead. Although she breathed and moved and spoke there was no vitality left in her. She was defeated, hopeless, a puppet whose strings had been cut, a sailor cast adrift in a hostile sea, a lost soul. Yet, he told himself, there was no need for any of this. This was an innocent. Of that he felt sure. And it was his duty to save her—from "Justice", from "the President of the Immortals", above all, perhaps, from herself and the demons that possessed her.*

'*Yet he also sensed a steel within. She had not merely accepted her fate, she was determined to fulfil it, and in doing so to resist those who might try to alter what she believed to be her destiny. No matter that there might be a man such as Tranter Reuben who believed in her innocence and was determined to prove it. She had set her heart against such interference.*'

Tudor looked enquiringly at his pupil.

'What do you think?'

'What I think,' said Elizabeth, 'is that you, and by extension your great detective, are smitten with Tess and with her plight and that you have convinced yourselves that she didn't murder Alec despite all the evidence to the contrary and her own admission of guilt. And I'd say you were on a hiding to nothing.'

'Well, you're right about one thing.'

'Which is?'

'That I don't think she did it.'

Elizabeth pursed her lips. They were in Henchards drinking mineral water because it suddenly seemed like a novel idea.

'You can't change the end?'

'What: Angel Clare and Liza-Lu on the hill watching the black flag go up over Wintoncester gaol and realizing that this means Tess has been hanged?'

'Yes.'

'I can do what I like. Just like Hardy. For the purpose of his book he is the President of the Immortals. He's the boss. Now he's out of the way I can do what I like. I'm President of the Immortals. Watch this space.'

'I don't think so.' She took the lemon slice out of her glass and sucked on it for a moment. 'You can add,' she continued, 'but I don't think you can subtract. You can't say that Tess lived happily ever after because we know she didn't. If there was a scene in which we actually saw Tess plunge the knife into Alec's stomach you'd have to accept it. The point surely is that there is no such scene. We don't know any more about what really happened than the landlady downstairs.'

It was Tudor's turn to muse.

'It's possible to rewrite history,' he said, 'eventually. In fact, you could argue that that's the whole point of history and historians. Each generation puts its own interpretation on the events of the past and invests them with a new meaning which accords with their own prejudices.'

'Ah yes,' she said, with a little smirk of triumph, 'you can change your interpretation of events but you can't change the events themselves. Take the Holocaust. It's historically permissible to argue that what happened to the Jews in Germany was a good thing. Disgusting but historically OK. But what you can't do is pretend it never took place. Same with Tess. You can argue that she didn't deserve to hang, but you can't claim that she survived.'

'You reckon?'

'I reckon.'

'I think you just made it up.' He smiled. He liked bantering with the child, though child in so many respects was just what she wasn't.

'Go on,' she said, 'read me some more. Then I'll tell you whether you're breaking the rules.'

They were almost the only people in Henchards and no one seemed interested in an eavesdrop. Nevertheless he read softly, not much more than a whisper.

' "The horse," said Reuben. "It was the horse that began it."

'Tess's eyes flashed momentarily and for a second she almost came alive. "The horse!" she exclaimed, "what do you know of the horse?"

'Reuben smiled softly. "I know little of the horse beyond the fact that he was named Prince, that he was essential to your father's business as a haggler, that very early one morning you were driving to deliver beehives to Casterbridge market with the horse in harness when you drifted off to sleep and the horse and cart drifted to the wrong side of the lane so that the morning mail-cart, advancing at speed on your unlit equipage, collided with you and yours, impaling the wretched Prince on his sharp shaft, thus causing the animal's almost instant death.'

' "Stop, stop!" The poor girl's hands were at her ears trying to block out the words. Her distress was extreme and far more evident than any remorse or sadness she might have felt for the late Alec D'Urberville. It was clear that whatever she felt about Alec she felt far more keenly for the horse. It was, of course, a characteristic of British womanhood to care more for their animals than for their menfolk.

'He stopped and she lowered her hands. "It is true," she said, "I felt like a murderess. Poor

161

Prince who was the only one who really toiled to help our family earn a living wage. It was all my fault. I felt like a murderess and still do to this day. There is blood on my hands. And that death meant oblivion and ignominy for my family too. I am bad, bad beneath contempt."

And she raised her hands but this time she put them to her eyes as she wept tears of despair and contrition, not for the demise of her husband, the father of her only child, but for Prince, the family horse.

'Reuben remained silent, watching with sympathy and compassion. When, after several minutes, she finished her sobbing, she looked up at him and asked, "But how did you know? About poor Prince, I mean. It is so many years ago. And though for us it was of the utmost, utmost significance, for a grand gentleman from London it must have been nothing. You could not know about such an incident."

'Tranter Reuben needed Tess to believe that he was omniscient, that he was indeed a truly Great Detective. So he was not going to admit that his informant was the elderly and infirm vicar of Emminster, the Reverend Clare, father of Angel. It was the old vicar whose sermon had effected the unlikely conversion of Alec D'Urberville into a born-again Christian, who so very briefly had been father-in-law to Tess herself" '

'Hang-on,' said Elizabeth, "born-again" is a solecism. Nobody would have talked about "born-again Christians" in the 1890s. Not even a Great Detective.'

'I think occasional solecisms are acceptable. Maybe even desirable. It reminds us all that this is a fresh contemporary take on the murder of Alec D'Urberville, not simply some sort of pastiche.'

Elizabeth looked unimpressed, but simply said, 'Do you think we could have something other than this mineral water? It's putrid.'

It was the turn of Rymills. Tudor ordered two glasses.

'Anyway,' he said, 'that's a stylistic detail. The point is that he's trying to win Tess over with a display of Great Detection. She is amazed that he knows so much about the death of the family horse. As she says, it was a cataclysmic event for the Durbeyfields or D'Urbervilles but hardly a blip on the seismic scale for a man-about-the-metropolis such as Tranter Reuben. If he knows every last detail about the horse's death then she'll expect him to know as much about the death of D'Urberville.'

'Hmm,' she said, 'I'm not convinced. She's got a death wish. She's not going to be deflected. Even if he persuades her that he's a good guy, in which case he'd be the first genuinely well-disposed male she's ever met, then the only help she wants is help to shuffle off this mortal coil because she hates it. I mean, give me a break. The girl kills her dad's

163

horse which means they're destitute; then she's seduced by the local cad who's a phoney aristocrat; she has his child which then goes and dies; she has to work her fingers to the bone ploughing the fields and scattering; then she rediscovers the love of her life and marries him only to blurt out the story of her rape or seduction, whereupon he acts all upset and disgusted and buggers off to Brazil, leaving her to fend for herself once more, and then the vile Alec turns up again, bribes her into marriage by offering to look after her widowed mum and her ten siblings, as well as saying that Angel's as good as dead and will never come back. But, of course, he does, and Alec, who is a complete shit, abuses her throughout the marriage and then taunts her about Angel. And it transpires that in any case Angel isn't really interested in her any more but prefers her Lolita-like younger sister. Well, if all that happened to you, you'd want to shoot yourself, wouldn't you?'

'Yes, but—' said Tudor.

'No buts,' said Elizabeth vehemently. 'She wants out. She knows Angel wants Liza-Lu but he can't have her while Tess is alive. Tess knows this but she's so brain-washed that she actually says she wants them to marry and when he says something about her being his sister-in-law she says "people marry sisters-in-law continually about Marlott" which was probably true and probably still is true in places like Digby Matravers, but is about as bleak a remark as any woman could possibly make. So I don't care what you say and frankly no one gives a damn whether she actually knifed bloody Alec, because Tess is determined to get out. And I don't blame her. Pleading guilty is the best exit line she has.'

Tudor looked at her thoughtfully and sipped some red infuriator.

'You're telling me that whether or not she actually murdered Alec is immaterial.'

The girl looked thoughtful. 'In the sense that Tess is going to hang whether she killed him or not then, yes, it's immaterial.'

'But in the classic detective story or mystery we have to have a resolution. We need to know who is guilty and the guilty person has to be brought to justice. That's the rule.'

'But,' she protested, 'that's not how it is in real life. Nor in any other sort of novel. Things aren't tidy in real life. We all know that. It's all loose ends and grey areas. Hardy knew that in a way that Conan Doyle didn't.'

'Tranter Reuben is going to prove Tess's innocence if it's the last thing he does,' said Tudor stubbornly.

'Well,' she said, 'I'll be fascinated to see how he does it because I'll bet my bottom dollar he can't make Tess change her story. Why should she? I've told you she's heading for the exit and she's not going to be deflected.'

'You could be right,' said Tudor after a very

long pause. A group of Casterbridge County Football Club supporters, in woolly hats and scarves, came in and ordered lagers all round. One of them burped loudly. His friends sniggered and they all looked across at Tudor and Elizabeth in a way which suggested class hatred and might, later at night and after a few more lagers, have become ugly. Tudor and Elizabeth studiously ignored them.

'So there's really no point in continuing this interview.'

'I don't think so, no.'

There was a chorus of 'Oggy, oggy, oggy, oi, oi, oi' from the far end of the bar.

'Time to go,' said Tudor.

'It's not even seven yet,' said Elizabeth, 'and I haven't finished my glass.'

'Five minutes max,' he said.

She nodded. 'I think you have to wrap up this session pronto,' she said. 'It's not going anywhere. She's not going to change her story. Probably not even if she's confronted with incontrovertible evidence. And Reuben doesn't have evidence, let alone incontrovertible. The horse isn't evidence even if it's interesting. By the way, how did Reuben know about the horse?'

'The vicar of Emminster,' said Tudor broodily. 'He's consumed with guilt. Guilt about his inadequate son; guilt about his false conversion of Alec; guilt about all the terrible things that befell Tess. After all, she was his

166

daughter-in-law. I think he shares Reuben's scepticism about the girl's guilt. That's why he wrote to Reuben and asked him to take the case on.

'You didn't tell us that,' she said accusingly.

'Didn't I? Well one has to play one's cards with a degree of circumspection.'

'So what now?'

Tudor glanced across at the football fans.

'Time to go,' he said, draining his glass, 'and as for Tranter Reuben, I think he's going to have to visit the scene of the crime. My guess is that the police have missed some crucial evidence. The Victorian police weren't terribly bright. Not nearly as bright as the great detectives.'

'There's nothing about that in the book'

'No,' said Tudor, ushering Elizabeth towards the door, under the leer of the lager-louts. 'You could say that Thomas Hardy was holding something back, concealing something material. If so, that would make him an accessory after the fact. I like the idea of the author in the dock.'

CHAPTER EIGHTEEN

The bus could not have got far. Indeed Cornwall was surprised that it had managed to get as far as it had. Its general decrepitude suggested terminal immobility. The D'Urberville charabanc manifestly belonged in an automobilian knacker's yard. It really ought to have stayed in the Stonehenge car-park as a sort of ancillary exhibit to complement the mysterious stones. The bus was, in its late mid-twentieth century way, every bit as sinister and enigmatic as the henge itself. After all, he mused, what happened to the man calling himself Al D'Urberville, was not so utterly removed from the human sacrifices which were popularly supposed to have taken place on the grey slab where Hardy's heroine spent her final night of freedom.

This time he did not take Elizabeth Burney and he did not liaise with Eddie Trythall. He had his reasons for operating alone and was not altogether proud of them. As a professional criminal academic he was dedicated to the notion that all crime could be explained and solved rationally and forensically. Yet the longer he practised the less sure he was of what he preached. Because so much crime was irrational, spontaneous or just plain mad, it seemed to him, increasingly, that it was not susceptible to police procedure. Murderers like Harold Shipman were beyond explanation. He supposed that some criminals could be understood, apprehended or even anticipated by cold, harsh logic. The terrorist or freedom fighter perhaps, but the suicide bomber, surely could not be understood by the normal, conventional, nine-to-five copper with kids and a mortgage. You couldn't get into that sort of mind without being a little mad yourself.

He didn't like to admit this to anyone but himself and indeed scarcely articulated the idea even as an interior monologue. To do so would have involved the destruction of everything that underpinned his life's work. He couldn't aspire to serious academic status if he thought you could achieve results on a whim and a prayer. Gut reaction wasn't good enough for a Reader in Criminal Studies. And yet today he was doing little more than playing a hunch. He wanted another word with the vicar's wayward son and he wanted it alone. He wanted answers but he wasn't sure that he knew the questions. And that wasn't something he was going to admit to a professional policeman or a precocious PhD. candidate.

He began where he had left off, in the car-park at Stonehenge. There was, as he had expected, no bus. One of the attendants told him that the vehicle had left the previous morning, earlier and turned north, belching smoke and coughing badly.

'Can't have got far,' he repeated, nudging the Morgan into the slipstream of a massive artic HGV, and ignoring the V sign from the driver of an unmarked white van immediately behind. The roads round Stonehenge had been a congested disgrace for as long as he could remember—a far cry from the 1890s when country girls could stride across the Plain with hardly another traveller in sight save perhaps a parvenu cad in a pony and trap. Tudor resigned himself to a mile or so in second gear and wondered whether those really were the days or not.

He had an idea about where the vicar's dropped-out son might have ended up. Latter-day travellers had a network of parking places dotted about the country which was as sophisticated in its way as anything provided by Michelin or even the Good Pub Guide. They were usually on land owned by a sympathetic farmer or squire prepared to turn a blind eye or better to the usually squalid appearance of these itinerants' temporary abodes. Either that or they were on common land where no single person had a coherent claim to ownership and where authorities were too scared or lackadaisical to move tramps, gypsies or other outsiders on their way. There was an estate a few miles north on the outskirts of Dormer Porcorum where a fey baronet called Sir Crispin Fell encouraged illegal raves and regular gatherings before the summer solstice knees-up at the henge. Tudor had a hunch—that dreaded word again—that young Lillywhite would be hunkering down there.

And so it proved.

170

The charabanc was parked in a clearing surrounded by a herd of Jacob's sheep who were chewing away at the grass apparently oblivious to the mangy German shepherd attached to the door-handle.

Tudor parked on the verge, walked towards the bus and was surprised when the door was opened by a late middle-aged woman with jangly ear-rings. It was the ear-rings that he noticed first though his second glance made him realize that it wasn't just the ears that were adorned with jangly bangles. She shall have bangles wherever she goes, he said to himself. The woman had big bracelets, a big string of ethnic knobs round her neck and she was wearing what appeared to be a mauve bell-tent, designed, Tudor guessed, to disguise a figure that had gone literally pear-shaped. She was smoking a cigarette in a long black holder and had a face almost as wrinkled as that of the poet W.H. Auden in old age. She looked like a fat tortoise in a wig, her hair manifestly having come from somewhere other than the top of her head.

'Yes?' she said, in a tone of voice which conveyed disdain and distrust and utterly belied the affirmative monosyllable. She said 'yes' but she meant 'no'.

'I'm looking for Mr Lillywhite,' said Tudor.

'So?'

The woman appeared to be speaking not so much down her nose as out of it. The second

171

monosyllable came at him like a bullet. In fact, had he not believed it to be a physical impossibility, he would have said that her nostrils were rifled.

'Is he in?' asked Tudor, striving to be on equal terms but feeling already as if he were playing catch-up.

'What's it to you?'

Tudor tried to stay cool.

'If he's in I'd like to talk to him: if he's not in I'll wait till he gets back.'

The woman looked at him as if he were a discarded crisp packet.

'Where are you from?'

'What's it to you?' he responded, feeling that the exact repetition of her earlier question at least gave him a point or two.

'What it is for me,' said the woman, 'is that I decide who Lillywhite talks to and who he doesn't talk to. I am Deirdre Robinson from *Wotcha!* and my magazine has acquired exclusive world rights to the Lillywhite story!'

Tudor was obviously supposed to have heard of Deirdre Robinson of *Wotcha!* He *had* heard of *Wotcha!* but had never read a copy. He knew only that it was a blokish magazine designed to emulate other blokish magazines such as *Loaded* and *Nuts.* It was aimed, more or less, at the younger generation of London taxi-drivers. Of Deirdre Robinson he had heard never a whisper.

'What story?' asked Tudor, owlishly and

disingenuously.

Deirdre Robinson blew smoke down her alarming nostrils.

'Since you ask I haven't quite decided,' she said. ' "Three in a bed sex romps" will come into it. So will "The murderous mistress". "I still love my son" says Vicar.' Deirdre inhaled and blew out more smoke. 'I must work in the little sister but I'm not sure whether to play her as a scheming Lolita or the innocent victim. Anyway, who are you? Are you from Social Services? If you're from *Bloke* magazine or one of the others, you're too late. It's all signed up. I'm just doing the interview and stopping him talking to anyone else. Follow me?'

Tudor said he followed. Deirdre was standing between him and the door to the bus and the dog was growling. He had been in stronger positions.

'You haven't told me where you're from. Or who you are,' she said, frostily.

'He's Dr Tudor Cornwall from the University of Wessex,' said a voice from the bus. It was Lillywhite. He was wearing black hobnail boots, army surplus fatigue trousers, and a grubby vest. He had a swastika tattooed on his right shoulder and did not appear to have shaved since Tudor had last seen him.

'Who's he when he's at home?' the woman from *Wotcha!* wanted to know.

'He runs the Department of Criminal

173

Studies,' said Lillywhite. 'My dad's been to his lectures.'

'Is that right?' asked Deirdre.

'Yes,' said the vicar's son.

'Cool,' she said, eyeing Tudor from head to toe and back again. She did not look impressed.

Another figure appeared in the doorway of the bus. This was a waif-like female in a man's shirt and bare legs. She seemed to be rubbing sleep from her eyes. Or maybe tears. She had a stud through her top lip, her left nostril and three through her right earlobe. Her hair seemed to have been Cherry-blossomed into black spikes.

'Are you Tess's sister?' asked Tudor.

Deirdre spoke for her 'Maybe. Maybe not. Frankly I don't think it's any of your business. Unless perhaps I put you in the story. What do you give degrees in? Pick-pocketing? Fraud? GBH? A Master's in Manslaughter. Maybe my guys were studying under you. "Taught to kill among dreaming spires", "A Master's in Murder", er . . . "Subsidised stabbing scandal".' She tapped ash from the cigarette holder and fluttered caterpillar-Cartland eye-lashes at him. 'What do you think?'

'I think I want to speak to Mr Lillywhite.'

'That's for me to decide,' she said, 'and right now the only people Mr Lillywhite is going to speak to are the million and a half readers of *Wotcha!* Buy a copy of next month's issue and

174

you'll be able to read all about it.' She grinned. 'So, on your bike, old man!'

The epithet 'old man' was not intended as a term of endearment. He guessed that Deidre was at least as old as he was and not half as well preserved. Too much gin, too many fags.

'I don't imagine you're the sort of hack who lets the facts get in the way of a good story,' he said.

Her eyes narrowed which meant that the twin caterpillars splayed on to the wrinkled bags beneath them. The intention was threatening though the effect was merely grotesque.

'You should be careful saying things like that,' she said, 'I've got witnesses.'

'And do you honestly imagine for a moment,' said Tudor, 'that any judge or jury would pay the slightest attention to whatever testimony these two are likely to produce?'

He realized the minute he said 'testimony' that he was in danger of sounding pompous and priggish. He knew this was a danger for him and could never quite understand it. He never felt pompous or priggish within, but sometimes that was how he seemed to others and he knew that he could be let down by his vocabulary and his tone of voice. Too many years of teaching pupils he didn't consider up to speed, he supposed. Almost without knowing it he had consigned all three of those in front of him to that category and they knew

175

it. It didn't matter that he was right, it was not a clever thing to have done, especially to Deirdre from *Wotcha!*

She looked at him as if he were even worse than the empty crisp packet she had identified earlier.

'You should know better than to mess with a free Press,' she said. 'We've paid good money for this story and we'll make really, really certain that the story we have is a really, really good one. And no two-bit, tin-pot, imitation academic is going to get in the way of that.' She flicked the cigarette from the holder, rammed another into it and lit it from an old-fashioned Zippo lighter.

Tudor looked from one to another of this ill-assorted trio and they looked back at him. He felt he had seen a surfeit of Zippos in the past few days.

He thought of repeating the line about power without responsibility being the prerogative of the harlot through the ages but decided against. Whatever he said, he was not going to get anything out of them. The inadequate Lillywhite, the Hell's Angel from Clare, and his nymphet girlfriend, had been well and truly nobbled. Even if they recognized the truth they were not going to tell it, least of all to Deirdre Robinson. It wouldn't have happened a hundred years earlier. What was it H.L. Mencken had said about the purpose of journalism? That it was meant to afflict the comfortable and comfort the afflicted. Something like that. He couldn't see that Deirdre Robinson and *Wotcha!* would pay much attention to that, though he supposed that in their way Lillywhite and the girl were among life's afflicted, and that the magazine's doubtless clinically obese cheque would at least pay for dope, drugs, alcohol and whatever else contributed to that affliction.

Tudor told himself he would never solve this mystery by just standing there. He wanted to shout out 'Whatever happened to truth?' but he knew that this would seem absurd and confirm their impression of him.

Deep down he felt his hunch confirmed. The vicar's son was so weak and unpleasant that he had to have been Al's murderer. Killing one of his erstwhile partners and putting the other behind bars left him free to pursue the little sister, drive the bus and walk the dog. Tudor felt he had a motive of sorts but he had no proof. Deirdre would certainly not let anything as old-fashioned as truth and justice get in the way of her story and all three would swear that it was the truth, the whole truth and nothing but the truth even though the world believed it to be a tissue of lies.

Tudor took one last look, disgusted as much by his own failure as by the three conspirators, turned on his heel and walked back to his car. He knew in his gut that he was right but he also knew that he could never admit that his heart said yes while his head said no.

Maybe I should stick to teaching, he said to himself. I'm just as guilty as that foul woman. My theories are just as dubious as her stories. We both play fast and loose with the facts. Whatever they may be.

CHAPTER NINETEEN

The class seemed in higher spirits than the week before. Tudor was inclined to put this down to the fact that the weather was fair and sunny and that England had just won an emphatic victory in an Association Football match. True, this was only against Latvia but any victory by the England football team was good for national morale in general and student morale in particular. Harold Wilson always believed—or affected to believe—that England's victory in the 1966 World Cup was the major factor in Labour's General Election victory. Tudor thought this fanciful and had caustic views on Wilson not least because of his paranoia about the Intelligence Services. He had written a light-hearted paper on the subject entitled 'The Man in the Gannex Mac', a reference too old to have much point any longer, but topical and apt at the time. There was no point in trying it out on the class. This generation had no sense of history, even of contemporary history. At least that was his view based on the students they were getting at Wessex. Perhaps other universities were luckier.

'As I recall,' he said, clearing his throat and bringing his thoughts back to the matter of the D'Urberville murder mystery, 'I asked you to answer a number of questions at the end of last week's session. Namely—did Tess kill the horse? Was the horse's death responsible for the ruination of her father? Did this mean that she had thereby dragged her family into a quagmire? Did her mother's solution to the family's misfortunes have an ulterior motive? What was the significance of D'Urberville's father's real name; had he been a money-lender oop north and was this significant? And did Alec's and Tess's physical appearance determine their characters and did this, in turn have any relevance to their sticky ends? I think that's more or less it.'

He paused and gazed round the room in a seemingly abstracted manner until he lit on the languid form of fairly aristocratic Freddie, characteristically sprawled on the table in front of him and apparently half asleep.

'Freddie,' he said, pouncing.

'Yes, sir,' said Freddie, grinning because he knew the pseudo-obsequiousness would annoy Tudor as usual. Tudor ignored him and instead asked him with what he hoped was icy politeness if he mind awfully reading his essay out loud. Freddie made no protest and read a perfectly respectable piece of work. In it he declared that Tess could have been responsible for killing the family horse in that she fell asleep at the reins and was on the wrong side of the road when the postman came careering along on his early morning rounds. On the other hand you could argue, plausibly, that her father should have performed the errand in question but was unable to do so on account of having taken excessive drink. So, if you were being fair, you'd have to say that the blame was just as much her dad's fault as hers. By the same token, although the death of the horse meant that her dad wasn't able to ply his trade of haggling, which depended on a horse-drawn vehicle to convey goods about the Wessex countryside, you could also argue that the family's affairs were in a parlous state already on account of old man Durbeyfield's alcohol abuse. The same thing applied to the 'quagmire' question. Yes, you could plausibly argue that the Durbeyfields were in, as Freddie put it, 'deep do-do' but you couldn't blame it all on the demise of poor Prince, let alone Tess. They were in a mess because the parents obviously didn't practise proper birth control. There were too many of them. And the old bloke was a serious no-hoper. No good at anything, not even haggling. That didn't stop Tess blaming herself but that was in her temperament anyway. She was the sort of girl who would always blame herself. One of life's victims. Consumed by feelings of guilt whether deserved or not.

Tess's mother didn't actually say out loud that she hopes her sexy daughter would appeal to young Alec but it was implicit, argued Freddie. Hardy made it very clear to the reader that she was that sort of mother. She saw her daughter's looks as the way out of their troubles. She would marry money and the most obvious source of money was the D'Urberville family. They were the only money the working-class Durbeyfields actually knew.

The fact that Alec's dad changed his name to make himself seem grander than he actually was suggested inherent dishonesty which would probably be passed on to his son. We didn't know that he was a money-lender but Hardy would have sown the seed in order to suggest further dishonesty. Hardy wouldn't have liked money-lenders, or northerners. In fact Hardy, despite or maybe because of his lower-middle-class southern origins, was pretty snobbish and this was reflected in the books. Physical characteristics: yes, he used them to suggest character, so we were told that Tess was young for her age and that 'phases of her childhood lurked in her aspect' even though only a small minority, mainly strangers, would notice this. Most people just thought 'she was a fine and picturesque country girl, and no more'. As for Alec, he was a sort of stereotype pantomime villain, the sort of bloke the audience hissed as soon as he appeared on stage: *he had an almost swarthy complexion, with full lips, badly moulded, though red and smooth, above which was a well-groomed black moustache with curled points, though his age could not be more than three- or four-and-twenty. Despite the touches of barbarism in his contours, there was a singular force in the gentleman's face, and in his bold rolling eye.* This was Flashman to a T.

Freddie's conclusion was that Alec was a cardboard villain and Tess a cut-out victim, and that it was patently obvious that the villain was going to have his wicked way with the victim. It is less predictable that he would come to a sticky end in a seaside guest-house and not, on the face of it, likely that the victim would turn on him, much less murder him. Yet we see near the beginning that Tess was a girl of spirit even though that spirit was usually subdued.

On balance Freddie said he didn't believe in the characters nor the story and least of all its final resolution.

'Not bad,' said Tudor, 'beta query alpha.' Beta query alpha was one of his favourite marks. It meant that the work was competent second grade stuff with a tantalizing hint of something slightly superior.

'What do the rest of you think?' He looked round at the class. 'Tamsin?'

'I think it's Victorian melodrama with mildly pre-feminist overtones,' she said.

'Is that what you say in your essay?'

'More or less,' she said. 'It's all so dated. It couldn't happen now.'

'Why not?'

This was Frances. She didn't mean 'why not?', she meant she didn't agree.

'You couldn't be as much of a loser as Tess,' said Tamsin, 'Not nowadays. And if you were as shitty as Alec you'd be banged up. There are laws to protect women from shitty blokes like him. Social services would step in and take the little D'Urbervilles into care. Tess would never be able to marry D'Urberville when there was no evidence that her first husband, Angel Clare, was dead. She'd be done for bigamy.'

Freddie disagreed. 'The news is full of losers like Tess,' he said. 'They get gang-raped in glitzy hotels by professional footballers. People like Alec D'Urberville. If he came back today he'd be the striker for some football club.'

'Not a very good one,' said Karl. 'He wouldn't have been a Man U or Arsenal bloke. More like Stockport County or Carlisle. Maybe not even a League club.'

Tudor wasn't sure that discussion of which football club Alec D'Urberville would have

183

played for had he been beamed back from the pages of a nineteenth-century novel was really part of the class's remit. On the other hand it was refreshing to find them having an animated discussion about anything at all. He didn't want to put a stop to it even if he felt it should be channelled.

'Do we think Alec is a crook? Or just a nasty piece of work?'

Eventually Tudor took a vote on this one and found the class divided down the middle— a fifty-fifty score with the girls tending to take Alec's side more than the boys. The girls seemed to think that Tess was asking for what she got. She wanted to be messed around. She was one of nature's masochists. The boys, however, felt sorry for her which everyone agreed, was what Hardy intended.

'Cecil Day-Lewis, in his introduction to the Collins edition of *Tess* thought Alec was "absurd",' said Tudor. 'He says he was "the conventional bold, bad seducer of melodrama: he actually twirls his moustaches and says 'Ha, ha, my Beauty.' " Do we agree?'

'Yes,' said Freddie.

'No,' said Frances.

'All right,' said Tudor, 'we don't agree about Alec but what about Tess? Day-Lewis says that she's "Hardy's most exalted vision of all that love could be". Tamsin thinks she's a chronic wet-blanket. How could Hardy believe her to be an exalted vision of what love could be and yet apparently believe her cold-bloodedly to have plunged a carving knife into her husband's stomach. Some Victorian readers were outraged.'

'That's because they were Victorian,' said Karl. 'If you put frilly fabrics round chair legs because it would be immoral to expose them then you're going to think Tess is immoral and evil.'

'Did Hardy think she was immoral and evil?'

Everyone seemed to agree that Day-Lewis was right in the sense that Hardy's sympathies are entirely with Tess, but the more they talked the more dubious the class seemed to become about the plausibility of both the characters and the plot. A diminishing minority argued that Victorian England was unrecognizable to students living more than a century later but an increasing majority of the class appeared to believe that the story was implausible even in late Victorian England.

'What would you say,' asked Tudor, 'if I were to say that a story very like *Tess of the D'Urbervilles* had actually taken place not a million miles from here and not a million minutes ago?'

There was quite a lot of laughter at this. Not particularly mirthful laughter, being more sneering or derisive.

'It wasn't real *then*,' said Freddie, 'and it isn't real *now*. That doesn't make it a bad

185

book, it simply means it's not a realistic book. Tolkien doesn't write realistic books. Harry Potter's not real. Same applies to Hardy. He's a fantasist but he's been mistaken for a realist. That's not his fault, it's the fault of generations of critics and readers.'

'Just suppose then,' said Tudor, 'that someone became fixated with the story of Tess and decided to live it out. Would that be possible?'

The class seemed perplexed by this.

'Truth being stranger than fiction,' he continued, 'it should be possible to take any fictional crime and carry it out in real life in such a way that it becomes odder, more bizarre, more unlikely, in a word more unrealistic than in the orginal make-believe.'

The silence that ensued seemed somewhat stunned.

'You're saying that you could take Alec D'Urberville's murder off the printed page and into real life,' said Freddie, 'and then, like, improve on it.'

Tudor nodded. 'Well put, Freddie. In fact I might even remove the query from your beta query alpha. I'd go further than that, though; I'd say that I think that it's been done. What's more if any of you had even an ounce of intellectual curiosity and read a newspaper occasionally then you might know what I'm talking about.'

'You can't believe what you read in the

papers,' said Tamsin. 'That's why we don't read them. It's not a lack of intellectual curiosity. Rather the reverse. If you're really curious and want to know what's going in the world the last thing you do is read a newspaper. Newspapers are just a lot of London wankers mouthing off at each other. Ignorant, vain and prejudiced. Why should I want to know what one of those people think about anything?'

Part of Tudor agreed with this.

'I'm not saying you should abandon any critical faculty when you read a newspaper. A healthy disrespect is perfectly acceptable. Ignoring them altogether is not. By the way, does anyone read something called *Wotcha!?*'

'Yeah,' said Karl. 'They give free copies to the Union.' Karl was membership secretary of the Union. 'It's sort of cool. Freaky. It's so untrue it sort of comes out on the other side if you know what I mean.'

'Not entirely,' said Tudor truthfully.

'Well,' said Karl, 'it's all lies but the lies are so whopping you end up kind of believing them so they become, well, like true.'

'So if you sold your life story to them, they'd get it all completely wrong, but in such an extreme way that they would end up getting it right.'

'Something like that. But you wouldn't want to sell your life's story to *Wotcha!*'

'Why not?' Cornwall wanted to know.

Karl shrugged.

'I'll bring a copy next time,' he said. 'You can see for yourself.'

CHAPTER TWENTY

Tudor decided to send his great detective to the scene of the crime. It was late in the day but Tranter Reuben, like most great detectives, was late on the scene anyway. Great detectives almost always were. Unlike the lesser sleuths and gumshoes who were paid professionals at Scotland Yard, the Sûreté or some all-American cop-shop, great detectives were only called in when all else had failed.

Thus Tranter Reuben and his man Ledlow.

It was axiomatic that in affairs such as this the conventional forces of law and order were never up to the task and so it obviously was in this case. Tess's confession had been, in effect, taken at face value. The testimony of Mrs Brooks, proprietress of The Herons guest-house, would be taken as more or less corroborating what Tess herself had said and the only other material witness was, well, dead.

In the normal course of events that would have been that: a classic marital tiff ending tragically because of the immediate proximity of a lethal knife. It would have passed virtually unnoticed save by those most immediately concerned had it not been for the intervention of Tranter Reuben. It was the same with Holmes, Wimsey, Campion and Poirot and even years later with Wexford and Dalgleish. True, these famous seekers after truth solved mysteries but without them there would never have been a mystery in the first place. The police would have grasped the most obvious solution, pronounced it the real one and convinced everyone else that they had, with a minimum of fuss arrived at the truth, the whole truth and nothing but the truth.

Great detectives didn't work like that. They saw mystery where everyone else saw simplicity; they made the straightforward convoluted.

Tudor wrote:

'I fancy this must be the place, Ledlow,' said Tranter, adjusting his flowing cloak and pushing back his wide-brimmed hat. We are looking for a "stylish lodging-house" and though it stands in its own grounds with a small lawn, rhododendrons and other shrubs it gives no hint of being a commercial enterprise. Indeed it is so private in its appearance that it is the last place in which one would have expected to find lodgings. And this being so, why do you imagine that the Durbeyfields came here? Why, there is only a small sign saying "The Herons". Nothing about the place suggests that it would be suitable for Alec and Tess to lay their heads. Why, I wonder, should they have chosen this house in which to lodge? What brought them here? Was

*their presence at The Herons serendipitous? Or
was there some connection with Mrs Brooks at
which we can but guess? Come, let us see.'*

*Saying which he strode purposefully up the
drive and rapped on the front door with
his silver-headed stick. There was a perfectly
serviceable brass knocker which is what every
other visitor would have sounded, but Tranter
Reuben was not every other visitor.*

*There was no immediate response to his rat-a-
tat-tat beyond a barely noticeable twitch of a net
curtain (observed, predictably, by Tranter but not
by Ledlow) but just as he raised his cane for a
second assault on the door it opened to reveal
the mistress of the house in all her matriarchal
starchiness.*

*She was instantly dislikable; later Reuben and
Ledlow agreed on this emphatically, and agreed
furthermore that this would have been the rest of
the world's first impression too. It was the
expression that did it. This was forbidding,
gloomy and without an ounce of generosity or
humour. In some people this could have given a
false impression because it was fleeting but there
was nothing transitory about Mrs Brooks's
expression. It was fixed and obviously had been
for the whole of her fifty odd years. Because of
this the structure of her face had been
permanently affected. Lines had appeared and
they all ran downwards. The crows' feet which in
another character might indicate laughter, here
spoke emphatically of solemnity. Her eyes were*

flinty and her mouth malign.

Her clothing was black from head to toe and she wore her steel grey hair in a bun. As far as Reuben and Ledlow could see, she had no redeeming feature. She was just ghastly.

'Yes,' she said.

'I,' said Reuben, 'am Tranter Reuben and this is my man, Ledlow.'

'We're full,' said the harridan landlady 'No vacancies.'

She made as if to shut the door but Tranter, quick as a flash, interposed his cane between the door and its frame.

'We have not come for a room, madam,' he said, 'but for a word.'

She gave him a look which would have frozen a boiling kettle.

'I have no words for you,' she said.

'Not even for money?' he asked.

'And why would you pay me for words?'

'Because they might save an innocent life,' said Tranter, 'and because I perceive that you dispense no favours free.'

'How much?' she asked through her rat-trap of a mouth. She had her price and given her circumstances it was unlikely to be particularly high.

'A guinea to come into your parlour,' said Tranter, and, 'more guineas thereafter depending on the quality of the information you impart.'

'Two,' she said, 'in advance.'

Tranter sighed.

'Ledlow,' he said, 'pray be so kind as to advance Mrs Brooks a couple of guineas.'

Ledlow did as he was told and the men entered The Herons.

There was an elk's head in the hall, a ponderously ticking grandfather clock, a portrait of the Queen and a general air of antimacassar and mothballs. Mrs Brooks led the way into her sitting-room and Tranter glancing up at the ceiling, saw that the blood of the deceased Alec D'Urberville still stained the paintwork.

Mrs Brooks followed the detective's glance and said, without a trace of emotion, 'There was an accident. A man died. It was most unfortunate and reflects badly on the reputation of the house.'

'It was about the, er, accident that I wanted your words,' said Tranter, 'except that my understanding is that it was no accident, but that the gentleman concerned was killed on purpose. There was nothing accidental about it. But before we move on to the death of Alec D'Urberville I wonder if you could tell me what if any connection there is between you and Mr D'Urberville.'

The woman seemed to think for a considerable time. Then, perhaps thinking that the more remarkable her words the greater the reward, she said, 'Before moving to The Herons I was in service. I worked for a number of Wessex families.'

'Including the Stokes,' said Tranter.

She gave him a sharp, hostile look.

'Stokes they might have been up north but they were always D'Urbervilles in Wessex.'

'Quite so,' said Tranter. 'Whether they were Stokes or D'Urbervilles does not greatly concern me. What does concern me is your relationship with Alec. He was known to you and you to him. That is why he and his wife came to lodge here. The house is not advertised in any way. He would have needed some form of inside knowledge before coming here.'

'Mr Alec had been here before. He knew my discretion could be relied on.'

'So Mr Alec had been here with different women? With girlfriends? With women of ill-repute?'

'This is a respectable house,' said Mrs Brooks, angry now.

'Give her another five, Ledlow,' said Tranter.

Ledlow did as he was told and the woman snatched the money with an air of triumph.

'So you knew Alec D'Urberville from the time that you worked for the family. Would I be making an impossibly wild guess if I suggested that at some time in the past you worked also for the Clare family in Emminster where, of course, you would have encountered young Mr Angel and his brothers?'

Mrs Brooks managed to look decently incredulous.

Eventually she shrugged and said, 'I did work for the reverend gentleman and a decent, honest man he was. Which is more than I can rightly say for Mr D'Urberville—not wanting to speak ill of the dead.'

'I wouldn't have thought you were the sort of person who would wish to speak ill of the quick or the dead,' said Tranter disingenuously. 'But nevertheless it sounds as if you preferred the Clares to the D'Urbervilles and would I therefore be correct in inferring that you also preferred Mr Angel to Mr Alec?'

Had Tranter not decided that Mrs Brooks was incapable of such a transformation he would have said that her sallow complexion became suddenly suffused with pink. The woman clearly had what one might call a soft spot for Angel Clare, and a correspondingly hard one for Alec D'Urberville. It was not a line of questioning the detective felt obliged to pursue.

'So it was not chance that brought Mr and Mrs D'Urberville to The Herons? Nor Angel Clare?'

'I run a good class of establishment,' she said. 'Everything's clean and above board.'

'I'm sure it is, Mrs Brooks,' said Tranter, gently, though with a hint of iron fist within the gossamer glove. 'Both Mr Clare and Mr D'Urberville were obviously valued customers who valued you as much as you valued them. But, if we're being absolutely, ruthlessly honest you're telling me that you valued Mr Clare just that little bit more highly than you did Mr D'Urberville even though, I suspect, Mr

D'Urberville was a better bet from a financial, that is to say, commercial, point of view.'

Mrs Brooks said nothing. There was nothing much to say. She had liked the nice guy and not the nasty one. Perhaps she had vestigial traces of humanity after all.

'Angel Clare came calling shortly before the death of Mr D'Urberville,' said Tranter. 'Can you tell me anything about the visit?'

Mrs Brooks shook her head. 'He came to see her, not him.' she said.

'How did he seem? How did he look?'

'He was not as I remembered him,' said Mrs Brooks. 'He had a pallor about him. He was grown awful thin so the skin was falling off him. He had been in South America and had been unwell. Sick of a fever.'

'And what was said?'

'I don't know.'

'Don't know or won't tell?'

She said nothing. Tranter sensed that no amount of money would elicit any helpful response in this direction so he changed tack.

'Mind if we look upstairs?'

'Upstairs?' she repeated. 'I don't even know who you are.'

'I have told you our names but beyond that you don't want to know who we are,' said Tranter.

'Just say we're friends of the family,' said the normally silent Ledlow, reaching in his pocket for more guineas. They would never get upstairs without them. He handed over another five.

195

The woman shrugged.

'It's still a mess,' she said. 'The police said not to touch anything but that was days ago. They haven't been back. There's nothing to see.'

But she led them upstairs and into a living-room. There was a dining-table still set with cutlery, crockery and a white cloth spattered with what Tranter assumed was dried blood.

'I'll leave you to it,' said Mrs Brooks. 'I don't mind admitting this room makes me come over all queer. Gives me the creeps. I never cared for him but I don't like to think of him being done in like that. Especially not by someone he loved. According to his lights that is.'

She sighed and left, clutching her profits.

From the folds of his cloak Tranter Reuben produced a formidable magnifying glass through which, getting to his knees, he proceeded to conduct a thorough search of the light dung-coloured carpet which was stained with the same rusty brown dried blood as the cloth.

'Aha,' he said after a while, 'it is as I had hoped. We have evidence, Ledlow. Hard, incontrovertible, cast-iron evidence. There is enough on this floor to prove guilt and innocence conclusively. No confession even under oath can counter what I see through the glass not so very darkly.'

'And what exactly do you see, sir?' asked Ledlow, who was not as dim as he sometimes appeared but who was paid, partly, to go through the motions of stupidity if only to present his

196

employer in a better light. This also, it had to be admitted, was useful in that it enabled the great detective to bounce ideas around. In that sense Ledlow was there for target practice. He was like a blank wall against which Tranter could throw any number of balls in order to study precisely how they bounced.

'A boot, Ledlow,' he said. 'And unless I'm much mistaken, a Brazilian boot. The imprint on the carpet is distinct and clear. It is almost like a stencil. And it is written in blood. Which tells us what?'

Ledlow's response was clear and certain. 'If the footprint is a bloody one, then it must have been made after the murder. Which tells us that whoever was wearing these boots could have been the murderer.'

'There are no other footprints,' said Tranter. 'No woman's footprints. Only a man wearing boots from Brazil. I have it in mind to find those boots and I believe that when we find them we shall have found the murderer of Alec D'Urberville.'

CHAPTER TWENTY-ONE

Tudor Cornwall looked at his prize pupil and smiled. She had been foisted upon him during his disastrous Visiting Fellowship in Tasmania; his feelings about her were ambivalent but, on the whole, favourable. But he was not able, in truth, to separate affection and desire from intellectual appraisal. Difficult. He was fairly certain she was bright; he was absolutely sure she was desirable. The one got in the way of the other. It always did. All the same one had to strive for objectivity. Apart from anything else there were penalties attached to the alternative: loss of tenure, social ostracism, dismissal, disgrace.

He therefore looked at the ceiling when he asked, 'So? What do you think?'

He could sense her coquettish pout.

'Is there such a thing as a Brazilian boot?'

'Well,' he was blustering mildly, 'a Latin-American boot. High-heeled. Designed to make little men seem taller. Unusual in late nineteenth-century Wessex. Unique possibly. And there would be enough extra detail to identify the boot-print conclusively. Wear and tear. Little oddities in the tread.'

'So you're saying they're Angel Clare's.'

'They have to be. Surely.'

She licked her lips and pushed an errant strand of hair out of her eye. Tudor risked a peep and regretted it. He really must make his head rule his heart. Thou shalt not lust after your students—even post-grads.

'If you say so,' she said. 'None of this is in the original.'

'Of course not,' he said, 'that's the point. Hardy wasn't writing detective stories. He

198

didn't know how. That's why he missed so much. He took everything at face value. Even twisted evidence to suit his purposes. He was trying to make a point about the place of women in late Victorian society. About women as victims. Men as licensed shits. So he bent the rules and twisted the evidence.'

'You reckon?'

'I reckon.'

He did rather hate this university room of his, so bare, austere, over-lit, over-heated, so unconducive to intimacy or even warmth. He wanted to suggest an adjournment to Henchards but felt he shouldn't. Too much tutorial in the wine bar led to tongues wagging. This was a closed community in which everyone's business was everyone else's as well. Academe was notoriously bitchy and vindictive.

'So what next?' she asked.

'Reuben needs to get corroborative evidence to back up the bloody footprints. So he needs to find Angel Clare. With any luck he will have been too careless to dispose of his boots. His Brazilian boots. And with any luck there'll be some blood-stained garments somewhere about the place.'

'How does he find Angel Clare?'

'He goes to the rectory in Emminster and confronts Clare's old dad, the vicar. The old boy's a bit of a fruit-cake and the wife's potty about her little boy. Tranter will do his concerned, anxious, Tennyson cloak-and-funny-hat bit, and Angel's parents fall for it hook, line and sinker and tell Tranter that Angel is shacked up with little Liza-Lu in rooms somewhere or other. Probably Sandbourne. But not this time with Mrs Brooks at The Herons. Too expensive. Also Mrs Brooks knows too much.' He paused. 'All right so far.'

'I suppose so. I'll let you know when you get to the end of the story. I want to know how it ends.'

'I'm not sure I can change the end.'

'I don't see why not,' she said. 'You're changing practically everything else.'

'Not really,' he said, 'just examining the evidence more thoroughly. The basics are the same. Tess is seduced by Alec, marries Angel, marries Alec, Alec is stabbed to death, the President of the Immortals has his sport with Tess and finishes with her when the black flag is run up at Wintoncester Gaol. I'm not changing the salient facts—just introducing some detective work.'

'And a detective.'

'And a detective.'

'So Tranter and Ledlow find out where Angel is and they run him to earth. Then what?'

Tudor put his fingers together and raised his fingers to his pursed lips as if in prayer.

'They find the boots and trousers with blood

200

on them. Maybe a shirt. Or a poncho or something suitably South American?'

'But surely,' she said, 'Angel would have disposed of them. He's not stupid.'

'No,' Tudor agreed, 'but he's supremely over-confident. Tess has confessed; Mrs Brooks has given him an alibi. He's in the clear. The police are happy and so's he.'

'But he hadn't bargained on a great detective,' said the girl, grinning.

'Absolutely not,' he agreed.

She jumped up suddenly, smoothed down her skirt and shook her head, so that her hair momentarily fell over her eyes.

'I can't stand this room,' she said. 'It's so antiseptic. I'd rather be anywhere else. Even boring make-believe Henchards. Take me there, buy me a glass of wine and read to me.'

He did as he was told, putty in her hands, he realized. Like all good Englishmen when alcohol is suggested he looked at his watch and, seeing that it was after six o'clock, acquiesced, feeling feeble and foolish.

'How are you with cricket?' she enquired, in the street between the uni and the wine bar.

She never ceased to surprise him.

'Why ever do you ask?' he said. 'You've known me long enough to have found out by now. The fact that you haven't suggests a certain indifference, but why do you ask?'

'It suddenly occurred to me,' she said. 'It's a defining characteristic for a Pom, wouldn't you say?'

The street was cold and grey as so often and had a Victorian gas-lit feel to it.

'Sir Arthur Conan Doyle was a keen cricketer and not bad either,' said Tudor. 'He once made a century for the Marylebone Cricket Club against Scotland. Not many people know that.'

She giggled. 'You're quite cute sometimes,' she said. 'Did anyone ever tell you?'

'Not for a while,' said Tudor, truthfully. 'But then I never made a hundred for MCC against Scotland.'

'Would you have liked that?'

'What?'

'To have made a hundred for MCC against Scotland?'

'Every Englishman,' he said, 'would like to make a hundred for MCC. But not, I think, against Scotland.'

'Explain. I'm a girl.'

'You're not a girl, you're a Sheila,' said Tudor. 'You don't need to have cricket explained to you. You know Scots don't play cricket. They toss cabers and curl.'

'I thought Douglas Jardine was a Scot,' she said.

They had arrived at Henchards' front door. Tudor held it open with an exaggerated display of olde-worlde English courtesy.

'Girls aren't supposed to know things like that,' he said.

It was the turn of the Rymills.

'It's incredibly sexist to assume that girls don't like cricket,' she said. 'I've always had a crush on Ricky Ponting and I played. I could bowl a googly. Bet you couldn't do that.'

Tudor conceded that he could barely turn his arm over, let alone bowl a googly.

'You know that story about Tom Stoppard?' he asked.

She sipped and shook her head.

'He's supposed to have applied for the job of political correspondent on the *Evening Standard*. When Charles Wintour, who was the editor, interviewed him he asked if Stoppard was interested in politics. When he said yes, Wintour asked him if, in that case, he could name the current Home Secretary. Stoppard looked at him, aghast, shook his head and said, "I said I was *interested* in politics—not *obsessed*." Well, I think I'm like that about cricket.'

'Hmm.' She regarded him thoughtfully over the top of her glass. 'Is Stoppard keen on cricket?'

'I'm told so,' he said.

'Funny. He's a Czech really. I wouldn't think there's a lot of cricket in Prague.'

They held this thought in their heads for a while, then let it go without it being wholly resolved.

'OK,' she said, 'so tell me what happened. I'm dying to know. And yes, if you've got some stuff you can even read it to me. I won't be bored. Promise.'

The only other drinkers present were four ruddy-faced young farmers in hairy tweed jackets, jeans and muddy boots huddled, improbably, over a bottle of Veuve Clicquot. They didn't look like eavesdroppers.

'Well,' said Tudor, 'Tranter and Ledlow get Angel Clare's address from his parents in Emminster and then hurry off to Sandbourne where they find him and Tess's under-age sister Liza-Lu cohabiting in rented accommodation. Tranter engages them in conversation while Ledlow, who's pretty hot at this sort of thing, does a quick scurry round outside. He's a positive bloodhound and within a few minutes he's discovered the Brazilian boots in a garden shed together with a pair of light moleskin trousers and some sort of poncho-like shirt. All bloodstained. Confronted with this, Angel denies murdering Alec and produces some obvious cock-and-bull story about skinning rabbits. Tranter naturally isn't having any of this and he says he's hanging on to the evidence. There's a furious row and Tranter and Ledlow make off towards the main railway station with Angel waving his fists at them and shouting "thief!"'

'But,' said Elizabeth, 'no one takes a blind bit of notice.'

'That is correct,' said Tudor, sounding disconcertingly like Ann Robinson compering

"The Weakest Link." '

She frowned into her glass.

'Wouldn't he have destroyed the evidence?' she asked. 'Burned the trousers and the poncho? Chucked the boots in a lake? Pretty bloody lax to have them hanging about in the dunny.'

'Angel is pretty bloody lax,' said Tudor. 'In fact, if you ask me, he's got a screw loose. But the point is he's feeling supremely over-confident. He thinks he's got away with it. Alec's dead and dead men can't talk. Mrs Brooks who seems like the only witness who could damage him, has a more than soft spot for him so won't testify even if called. Or put it another way, she'll perjure herself if doing so gets him off the hook. And the clincher is that Tess has confessed. She's been under huge emotional pressure to do so but the jury don't know that. There's no legal aid so she's probably defending herself. Or rather she's not defending herself because she doesn't want to. She's defenceless as she's always been. Even Thomas Hardy is against her. He wants her dead just as much as anyone. Including herself.'

'Except,' said Elizabeth, 'that you've now invented a champion for her in the person of the great detective. Tranter Reuben is riding to our heroine's rescue on his white charger.'

'Yes,' said Tudor.

'So now what?' she wanted to know.

205

'Well,' said Tudor, 'the two men hurry through the streets of Sandbourne with the murderer's cries echoing in their ears. Reuben's cloak is billowing behind him in the wind. Little Ledlow is holding the evidence close to his chest and they're running to catch the last train to Wintoncester. Well, metaphorically speaking. Actually they're trying to catch the next train to Wintoncester and suddenly Tranter has this horrible feeling that they really are late coming to the case. Possibly too late. There isn't a moment to lose. And who knows, maybe Angel and Liza-Lu are in pursuit and maybe they will manage to convince people that they're in the possession of stolen goods, that Tranter Reuben has made off with his trousers. Which is, after all, perfectly true, even if they are covered in the dead man's blood.'

The four farmers, who had evidently struck lucky on the 4.30 at Southwell, were giving them peculiar looks and Tudor realized that in his excitement he had raised his voice.

'I'm sorry,' he said, 'I'm afraid I was getting rather carried away.'

'Like Angel Clare's clothing,' she said laconically.

'You're being facetious,' he said.

'Not in the least,' she said, 'but those guys over there think you're some sort of fruit-cake. They could well be right.'

'But what do you think?' he wanted to

know. 'Am I right? Did it really happen as I'm telling you? Have I filled in the gaps plausibly?'

She looked thoughtful. 'I'm not sure,' she said at last. 'It's legitimate to fill in the gaps but not to change the ending so I'm not sure I see where this is leading. But go on. Read to me.'

CHAPTER TWENTY-TWO

Tudor removed a sheaf of papers from his brief case, put on his reading glasses, ran a finger round the inside of the neck of his black polo-neck sweater, took a sip of wine, coughed, and glanced nervously across the table at Elizabeth. She smiled encouragingly and he started to read.

Tranter Reuben had what another author might have called 'Authority in the Abstract'. It was a quality impossible to define. His bulk, accentuated by the Tennysonian cloak and the wide-brimmed hat, might have had something to do with it; or the ferocious whiskers, not to mention the equally ferocious scowl that he habitually assumed when about to encounter someone or something that might seek to counter his own ambitions. The presence of Ledlow at his elbow was certainly a help in implying a status that he did not actually possess. Perhaps most important was a truculence which came naturally to him. He was used to getting his own way and because this was clearly important to him others less fierce in their ambition habitually caved in.

Elizabeth interrupted. 'Point of fact,' she said, 'the reference to "Authority in the Abstract" is a reference to Conrad's *Lord Jim* who was described as having "Ability in the Abstract" but *Lord Jim* wasn't published till 1900 which is ten years after *Tess*. So that's a literary solecism. Minus ten.'

'How did you know that?'

'We have a university in Tasmania, too, you know. Matter of fact, it's perfectly good.'

He sighed. 'OK,' he said, 'I'm sure you're right. But Conrad was already writing. He'd left Poland and jumped ship in the eighties.'

'But he hadn't written *Lord Jim*,' she insisted. 'Hadn't coined the phrase. Your timing's out.'

'Oh all right,' said Tudor irritably, 'I'll change it. I don't even know if Hardy and Conan Doyle and Conrad knew each other. If they did they might have nicked each other's ideas and phrases. Literary theft happens all the time nowadays. There's no reason to think that plagiarism wasn't around in Victorian England.'

'Oh just admit you're wrong and get on with

208

it,' said Elizabeth.

Her insistence didn't improve his temper but went back to reading.

Unfortunately the judge in the D'Urberville murder case was Mr Justice Ramsbottom. It was always unfortunate for most of those concerned when "Strawberry" Ramsbottom was in court. His real name was Arthur but he was known throughout the legal profession and beyond as "strawberry", firstly on account of his nose which was bulbous, purple and pitted with small black spots exactly like the eponymous fruit, and secondly because of the glass of "strawberry-ade" which always stood at his fingertips in court and which, though it contained a tincture publicly described as being no more potent than fruit juice, was actually alleged, on sound evidence, to contain a mixture of gin and Dubonnet in the proportion of approximately seven parts gin to one of Dubonnet. Mr Justice Ramsbottom was never exactly sober although even his enemies would be hard pressed to say that he was ever exactly drunk.

Mr Justice Ramsbottom was what was commonly known as a hanging judge. Some men—always men in those distant misogynist days—went into the law because they believed in truth and justice; others, almost certainly a majority, became lawyers because they wanted to boss other people about and if possible have them locked up, transported, or best of all, hanged. Flogging, drawing and quartering appealed to many of these men and, to them, it was a matter of regret that they were no longer in the legal repertoire.

For Strawberry Ramsbottom a juicy murder trial was a thrilling event and if the accused was found guilty and he was allowed to don the black cap and pronounce sentence with all that sonorous stuff about 'being taken from this place and hanged by the neck until dead' the thrill became positively orgasmic.

There was an interruption at this point.

'Point of fact, said the girl, 'late Victorians wouldn't have used the word "orgasmic". Certainly not in public.'

'Point taken,' agreed Tudor, 'though I think you'll find it was first used in 1684 but not perhaps in polite society. And certainly not polite Victorian society. Would you allow "sexual" instead?'

She considered this for a moment and then nodded. 'OK,' she said. 'Now proceed.'

Not for the first time Tudor found himself wondering who was the master and who the mistress.

It was no great problem for the imperious Tranter Reuben and his acolyte Ledlow to gain access to the courtroom. Security was lax and Reuben gave the impression of someone who had a right to be there. Nobody made a serious attempt to stop them until they found themselves in the Great Hall itself with the round table, reputed to have belonged once to King Arthur himself hanging, like the sword of Damocles from the wall.

Their entrance was greeted with an almost tangible silence. No one spoke: not the accused Tess, white and lachrymose in the dock; not my learned friends in the gowns and wigs; not the uniformed police; not the unblinking stiff-collared jurors; not the members of the public, crowded, prurient, in the public gallery; not even, at least for a moment, the strawberry-nosed Mr Justice Ramsbottom himself

For a few seconds the judge and the great detective eyed each other like bull and matador in the ring. Reuben's eyes narrowed; Ramsbottom's bulged. Reuben reached out for the incriminating Brazilian boots; Ramsbottom took hold of his glass of red liquid and raised it to his lips. Then the newcomers realized, with a frisson of horror, that the judge had donned the back cap. Reuben and Ledlow had interrupted Strawberry Ramsbottom in the act of condemning Tess of the D'Urbervilles to death on the gallows and His Honour was not pleased.

When he had taken a slug of what was obviously strong drink, the judge made a noise somewhere between a cough and a belch, shook himself like a hippopotamus emerging from the Limpopo, and glared at the two interlopers.

'Pray tell me,' he said, 'to what do I owe the unexpected pleasure of your company?'

211

Reuben did his best to glare back.

'I have evidence, My Lord,' he said, waving the boots at judge, jury and their learned friends.

Evidence was not something in which this particular judge was much interested especially if it interfered with a guilty verdict. Just as a certain sort of journalist never lets the facts get in the way of a good story, so Mr Justice Ramsbottom, did not lightly let evidence interfere with the maximum sentence.

'It is too late for evidence, Mr Reuben,' said Strawberry Ramsbottom. 'You are in contempt of court and I am passing sentence. However since you have interrupted the due process of law I shall pause to pronounce upon you and others of your ilk such as the infamous, so called great detective, Mr Sherlock Holmes. In doing so I am confident that I speak for all my learned friends both on the bench and in the courts. I am uttering truths and sentiments which are held by every member of my noble profession from the Lord Chief Justice himself to the lowliest pupil still eating his dinners at the Inns of Court.'

Reuben was not having this. He was not afraid.

'With respect, Your Worship,' he replied, 'I am here to see justice done. No man even if he sits where you sit wearing a full bottomed wig and a black cap is above the law. I am here in the service of the truth, and the truth, as I can prove, is that Tess D'Urberville did not murder her husband. She is as innocent as the lily

of the field.'

'This is my court, sir,' riposted the judge, 'and in my court I am neither above nor below the law for I am the law itself. All manner of men shall quail before me for I am the law, the law of our gracious sovereign the Queen, the law of God Almighty, the one and only law which shall not be gainsaid, not trifled with by some self-appointed sleuth who sets himself up as an investigator into matters which are no concern of his. You are a meddling menace, sir, and I shall have you put away.'

This was by no means the first encounter between the two but there had never been a confrontation such as this. Reuben was on dangerous ground. He had ventured on to enemy territory with no protection save his evidence which he chose to maintain was proof.

Counsel for the defence was a callow youth not long down from the university, he being the best that Tess's family and friends could afford. He had put a wretched defence, indeed had offered no defence at all, her plea of guilty being apparently unalterable, and had attempted only an appeal for understanding on the grounds of mitigating circumstances which he was at a loss to explain coherently, not least because of the frequent and sarcastic interruptions of the sceptical judge who had the scent of blood in his nostrils.

'My Lord,' he stammered, 'with respect I would be obliged—'

'Damn your respect and damn your obligation,' said the judge.

Tudor had toyed with the idea of having the judge 'thundering' but he was afraid the word was a little too penny-dreadful even if plain 'said' was on the weak side. He was quite sure that Strawberry's voice would have had a Vesuvial quality to it, a little like molten lava, helped out by a lot of gin and cigars.

'And damn you,' he continued, glaring at the great detective. 'You, sir, treat the law with contempt. You believe that you have a God-given right to interfere, to produce half-baked, highfalutin' ideas and theories to explain what has already been explained and what is perfectly clear to anyone with a ha'p'orth of common sense. You are a nuisance, sir. You make a mystery out of that which is not mysterious, you make complicated that which is not complicated, and above all you make innocent those who are not innocent. Here today, sir, you come to my court and seek to tell us that this murderess who has been found guilty of the most heinous of crimes by twelve good men and true according to the noble traditions of British justice is actually a wronged wretch who has never hurt a flea. Well, I have to tell you, sir, that you are mistaken and that you are a menace and I order that you and your flunkey be taken from this place to the cells below where you will cool

214

your heels until such time as you repent of your insolent folly and feel able to come back to this place and apologize, grovelling, for the inconvenience to which you have put us, and for the insult you have offered to this court, to Her Majesty, to the law and to myself.

It was clear which of these was the most important.

'But,' expostulated Tranter Reuben, who knew that he was right, that he was on the side of the angels, and that the judge was all piss and wind.

'I'll have none of your "buts",' said Ramsbottom. He motioned to the court officials standing ready, eager even, to do his bidding and bundle the two intruders to the damp squalor of the cells below.

Tranter Reuben made as if to resist, thought better of it, and let himself be manhandled from the court-room, allowing himself the slight recompense of fixing the judge with a beady eye and saying, 'You, sir, are not fit to sit in judgment on your fellow human. You are a man of no compassion, no feelings, no sense of what is right and wrong, and, moreover, you are drunk, sir.'

This last, in particular, was perhaps not such a good idea but the judge said nothing further, merely waited until his court was clear and then returned to the sombre matter of sentencing poor Tess to death by hanging.

Tudor looked up from his papers and waited.

'Is that it?' the girl asked.

He thought for a moment. Ultimately the scene lacked pzazz or oomph. He could see that. If it was to have real drama Tess would have got off. The great detective would have carried her off on his metaphorical white horse with the trusty Ledlow riding pillion.

'I'm hamstrung by Hardy's ending,' he said. 'Tess swings. I can't change that. President of the Immortals and all that. I can protest her innocence but I can't save her from the hangman's noose, that horrid black flag, Angel and Liza-Lu watching from the hill top. Ghoulish, I call that. The two of them watching to see that Tess's life is over so that theirs can begin.'

'You sure you can't change the verdict?' Elizabeth asked.

'I don't think,' he said, 'I need to formulate proper laws about fiddling with fiction: something along the lines of Monsignor Knox's diktats on crime writing. You know— no poisons unknown to medical science, no sinister Chinamen. But I feel quite strongly that you can rearrange and add but you can't alter substance or subtract. If Hardy has Tess found guilty and hanged then I'm not in a position to argue.'

'But if you came across a similar or even identical case years later, in real life, for the sake of argument, then that would be different?'

'Yes,' he smiled, 'that would be different.'
She smiled back.
'Good,' she said, 'I think it's different too.'

CHAPTER TWENTY-THREE

Tudor had not forgotten Deirdre Robinson, the woman from *Wotcha!* but he had set her aside.

It was not that she was forgettable—far from it—but she was someone he preferred to exclude from his consciousness and who seemed irrelevant to his main preoccupations. If she and her grubby little rag were prepared to fork out money for whatever story the Hell's Angel from Clare was prepared to fabricate that was her problem. Given that bargain-basement journalism was widely supposed to have well-established links with organized crime he had surprisingly little to do with it. Perhaps Eddie Trythall was right and he had no real taste for the sharp end of criminal activity. Perhaps he was frightened of it; was scared of becoming involved; scared of being threatened, roughed up, bumped off even. Such distancing from danger would fit his character. Involvement was not his strong suit and indeed he habitually argued that a certain detachment was essential in the serious academic and intellectual.

This, coupled with a definite fastidiousness, which did not always sit well with the world of criminal academe meant that he was a tad blinkered when it came to hacks from the red-tops and soft-porn glossies. He had met one or two, had even broken bread with them at the occasional award dinner or chief constable's drinks, but he had never got to know one, much less become a friend.

He supposed he was old-fashioned. He had been brought up to believe in a 'gutter Press' and in 'papers of record'. That distinction had become increasingly blurred and the gutter was more and more mired in muck. He preferred to have nothing to do with it.

In the matter of the D'Urberville Murder Part Two he didn't see that he'd anything whatever to learn from the woman at *Wotcha!* His dilemma was altogether more sophisticated than anything that magazine, its readers or writers, would comprehend. His problem, put simply, was what do you do when innocent parties insist on maintaining their guilt? How do you proceed when the guilty protest their innocence? What do you do when there is no real proof or evidence but when you know viscerally, emotionally, and even intellectually that things are not as they are going to pan out in court? How, in other words, do you prevent a miscarriage of justice when all concerned are determined that justice shall miscarry.

This had happened throughout history and to his way of thinking the police were part of the problem. It was partly why he was, unfashionably and in an out-of-date way, in sympathy with the amateur sleuth. The police, not in his estimation always blessed with brain, were always strongly biased in favour of conviction at all costs. It was part of their job to get villains put away in order that society, especially upper- and middle-class society, should sleep easy at night. The judiciary, like judges from the bloody-thirsty Jeffries who had caused so many innocent farm boys to be strung up after the Monmouth Rebellion right up through old strawberry nose in the first D'Urberville case and through to the grim authoritarians of the present day, were far less committed to law than they were to order. It was the job of someone like himself, someone in the tradition of the great detective, to redress the balance.

And in this case he knew he was right. The girl hadn't killed her man. She had given up on life, on men, on the world, but that did not make her guilty. Knowing that, however, was not enough. He had to convince others that he was right and he had to do so in the face of her own protestations of guilt. Was it possible to convince anyone, let alone a judge and jury, that the accused was innocent when she herself insisted she was guilty? Not easy, particularly when he was forced to admit that his own case

219

was based on belief and intuition rather than hard evidence.

Thoughts along these lines were not helpful when running a class. In fact, thoughts along any lines were not helpful when running a class and this was more than usually true when the class were being unhelpful. This morning they seemed to be in a curious, sniggering mood that he hadn't encountered before.

It was Karl who provided the explanation.

'The new *Wotcha!'s* out,' he said, 'so I brought it along for you to look at. I think you'll be amused by its presumption, as they say in the booze business.'

He stood up, fashionable holes in the knees of his jeans, hair spiked, cheeky grin playing round his steel-pierced lips and handed Tudor a glossy magazine with a front page of vibrant colour, asterisks and exclamation marks. Underneath the strident *Wotcha!* headline and the strapline which said 'World's Number One Magazine' the lead story was captioned PROFESSOR PORN EXPOSED. *WOTCHA!* NAMES THE DIRTY DOCTOR WHO MAKES CRIME PAY!! And there, unbelievably but unmistakeably, was a picture of himself, looking he had to admit, furtive, a bit seedy and a pretty plausible sex-fiend. Almost worse there was an inset picture of Elizabeth Burney alongside, wearing very little (amazing what digitally-up-to-speed art directors can do) above the heading 'TEACHER'S PET!!'

Had Tudor lapsed into wotchaspeak he would have said he was gob-smacked. The class, he was aware, was in a state of collective smirk or snigger though he also realized that their reaction was, to an extent, dependent on his own reaction. If he laughed it off they would do much the same; if he took it seriously then likewise. The worst scenario, of course, was that they might believe it, though an important part of what he was trying to teach them was that, within reason, they shouldn't believe anything they read in the papers, let alone in something like *Wotcha!* Young people today were extraordinarily gullible. His generation had been sceptical to a fault. He caught himself. He must try not to sound like the quintessential grumpy old man. It was counter-productive and not in character. He was neither grumpy nor old at least not in his own estimation.

Even so the magazine Karl had given him was enough to make the sunniest youngster turn gnarled and dyspeptic overnight.

He flicked the pages. There were a lot of pictures of notorious murderers such as the Wests, the Moors Murderers, the Kray Brothers; also women in various stages of undress, some alive, some dead, some mutilated. It was all more or less disgusting and he and his image seemed to be the only connecting link. He was on every page— sometimes the paedophile-looking snap that

221

he guessed must have been taken by the dreaded Deirdre or possibly the Angel from Clare or his little Lolita look-alike when he paid his second visit to the bus. He hadn't been paying attention.

'Is it always like this?' he asked eventually, looking at Karl but addressing the query to the class in general.

'Yah,' said Freddie in his most languid Old Etonian drawl. 'You gonna sue?'

'Do you think I should?' Tudor was regaining his composure but he still felt distinctly queasy. He did sometimes adopt a moderately high profile but always of his own making. Normally his head was below the parapet, deliberately so. This sort of publicity was unexpected and unwelcome.

'They're tricky to sue,' said little Celtic Tamsin. 'Everything in *Wotcha!* is fine-tooth-combed by really hot-shot libel lawyers. My sister's a barrister. She reads for them sometimes.'

Tudor gave her a sharp look as if to say 'You never told me, traitor.'

'If I don't sue everyone will assume it's true.'

'What's true?' asked Freddie. 'You haven't even read it yet.'

'I don't need to,' said Tudor. 'Professor Porn . . . Dirty Doctor . . . Tacky Teacher . . . Why would I want to read any further?'

'That's just vulgar abuse,' said Freddie.

'Like David Beckham calling the linesman a *hijo de puta*. Sticks and stones may constitute an offence in law but not words. You of all people should know that.'

Tudor, suddenly, didn't care for Freddie's tone.

'Academics can retain libel lawyers. They're not the prerogative of blokish men's glossies.' he said. 'What they've done is professionally and personally damaging. I think they'll be made to apologize. And pay money. Lots of it.'

'But,' said Freddie who had the bit between his teeth, 'it's actually quite clever of them because leaving aside the insults what they're actually saying is true.'

'Meaning?' said Tudor sharply.

'Meaning,' said Freddic, 'that running an academic so-called Department of Criminal Affairs gives you a licence to go poking around in other people's affairs to your heart's content. You have total freedom to jump into everyone's laundry basket and roll around in their dirty linen.'

'Power without responsibility,' said Tamsin, unexpectedly. 'The prerogative of the harlot throughout the ages.'

'Kipling,' said Tudor, seeking in what he knew was a slightly childish attempt to regain authority by a demonstration of superior knowledge. 'Later appropriated by Stanley Baldwin in order to attack the popular Press of the day. *Plus ça change.*'

223

He smiled a wintry smile.

The class looked sceptical.

'They have a point' said Karl. 'Like I don't like the capitalist bourgeois Press any more than you do, but you haven't been elected, you're not part of the police set up, you don't have any authority but you *can* mess around wherever you like being holier than thou, and because you've got academic clout everyone takes you seriously. *Now Wotcha!* has blown the whistle and called you a dirty old man who goes round stalking anyone he feels like under the cloak of academic respectability. Like I said, they've got a point.'

'If you believe that then what are you doing here studying for a Criminal Studies degree?' Tudor retorted, stung.

'I didn't say they were right,' said Karl. 'I just said they had a point. That's not the same.'

Tudor looked at the grubby pages of the grubby magazine. This, he thought, was the price of democracy. I disagree with what you say but I defend to the death your right to say it. He sighed.

'Listen,' he said, 'you know as well as I do that what we're doing here is not only legitimate but necessary. Crime, in all its many manifestations, is an integral part of society. It's the downside of the world; it's the devil's work; it's what stops our lives being happy and worthwhile. It has to be fought: it has to be defeated. In order to do that we have to understand the nature of crime. We have to understand the criminal. We have to understand wrong-doing, the underworld, the anti-social. To promote goodness and happiness we need to understand the enemy. You surely know that, or you wouldn't be here. This sort of journalism is part of the opposition. It represents every-thing that right-thinking people abhor but the minute you're confronted with it you succumb. You're suckered.'

He stopped. He was protesting too much. It was a rant as much as a considered argument.

'So what are you going to do?' This was Freddie, a pedigree dog returning to a champion bone.

'What would you do, Freddie?'

Freddie shrugged. 'I'd leave it, *you* know it's drivel. *We* know it's drivel. The hacks who wrote it know it's drivel. So who else matters?'

'The people who read the wretched magazine,' said Tudor. Not, he thought, unreasonably.

'Which means,' said Freddie, 'a load of gormless gits who know nothing, who don't matter, who don't count and who you're certainly not going to meet at dinner parties or even Henchards Wine Bar.'

Tudor swallowed hard.

'Well, thank you, Freddie,' he said. 'Very educational.'

225

He thought for a moment. What the woman had written had little or no bearing on the case. She didn't even mention Thomas Hardy let alone *Tess of the D'Urbervilles.* She gave no suggestion that there might be parallels between the fiction of 1890 and the facts of 2004. It was just scurrilous slagging off of 'pseudo-intellectuals'—people such as himself—who got their rocks off by poking around in the private lives of the Angel from Clare and the latter-day Liza-Lu—readers of *Wotcha!* magazine.

'I know,' he said, coolly, 'that this doesn't, strictly speaking, come under the heading of crime reporting, but I'd like you, Karl, to organize photocopies for the rest of the class and I'd like you to file it away, everybody, so that when we do crime reporting and court reporting next term we can see if it has any relevance. Remember that there are strict rules about reporting matters which are *sub judice,* that cases have been dismissed because of prejudicial reporting, that a certain sort of publicity means that the accused is unable to benefit from a fair trial. And so on. The whole question of journalism and the law is fascinating and complex.'

'But,' protested Karl, 'this *Wotcha!* piece doesn't prejudice any trial. It hardly talks about the D'Urberville murder; it's an attack on crap degree courses and so-called academics interfering in important matters of life and death which they don't understand and for which they have no authority.'

'You could argue that any kind of academic activity is invalid because it's removed from the reality of everyday life,' said Tudor. 'But, as we all know, that is its strength. Those of us who are privileged to work in universities can see the wood from the trees; we can see the shapes and patterns which ordinary people are unable to detect; we can make sense of what otherwise doesn't make sense. That's our job.'

'Which isn't how other people see it,' said Tamsin.

'Precisely,' said Tudor, with an air of triumph which was not as genuine as he made it sound. 'And now I think we've spent quite enough time on this sordid little magazine and should return to our studies. Though we'll come back to *Wotcha!* at a later date.'

The class seemed unconvinced.

So was he.

CHAPTER TWENTY-FOUR

The dining-room at Sandbourne's Imperial Hotel had been given a make-over. Whereas it used to be simply The Dining-Room with candelabras and red carpets, it was now called Viceroy's. The waiters, still the motley collection of assorted illegals speaking no known language, moth-eaten old retainers, drunks and assorted layabouts, had been kitted out in turbans, white pantaloons and waistcoats. The waitresses wore saris which didn't suit pallid, plump druggies from Eastern Europe any more than the pantomime gear of their male counterparts.

Actually, it wasn't as bad as all that, thought Tudor, nibbling a poppadom and contemplating a large 1933 black and white photograph of the Maharajah of Patiala and the England Cricket Captain Douglas Jardine on a tiger shoot, a few yards over Eddie Trythall's left shoulder. He was still smarting from the article in *Wotcha!* and from the certainty that he was right about the D'Urberville murders, both of them, but wasn't going to be able to persuade anyone else.

DCS Trythall was ordering a prawn cocktail followed by steak and kidney pudding except that the prawn cocktail was called Poona Prawn and the steak and kidney pudding Lord Curzon's Delight. Trythall, being Trythall, was too embarrassed to pander to the whims of the new image-makers and simply said, 'Prawn cocktail, steak and kidney pudding and a pint of Tally-ho!'

Steak and kidney pudding was just about his favourite food.

Tudor accepted the subcontinental theme to the extent of a samosa starter followed by

228

Chicken Madras (both given silly names which he couldn't be bothered with either) but departed from the script by asking for a glass of Chilean chardonnay.

'I've brought you the Deirdre Robinson file such as it is,' said Trythall, when their Latvian waiter stomped away scratching idly at the base of his turban I'm surprised you don't remember her. She was real trouble in those days. Different sort of trouble but still trouble. Funny how poachers turned gamekeepers lose their sense of humour along with everything else. Reformed smokers, alcoholics anonymous, born-again Christians—sour buggers, the lot of them.'

Tudor supposed so though it occurred to him that he and Eddie were inclined to be sour buggers themselves these days. Odd that, they were both successful according to their lights, and yet they both had moments like these when they were aware of quickening years, of life passing by, things not being what they used to be when all was promise and lightness of touch. Tudor's problems, he reckoned, were to do with an emptiness—emptiness in his socio-sexual life which seemed to be seeping into his professional world as well. Eddie's worries were the opposite—overlong hours and too much humdrum work to fill them; nagging, unloving wife; financially and emotionally demanding children. Whatever the cause the result was the same in each case—creeping disillusion and a bleak dislike of most other people. They were both going through a crabby phase and today was a particularly crabby day.

'You read the piece?' asked Tudor.

'Skimmed it,' said Eddie. 'Par for the course. Deirdre's good at innuendo. Always was. Nudge, nudge. Wink, wink. No smoke without fire. Dangerous opponent. Not a good person to get on wrong side of. Looks as if you've done just that.'

Tudor snapped off another corner of poppadom and chewed it morosely.

'It wasn't intentional,' he said. 'She just got in the way. There she was in the bus acting as if she owned it and the pair of them. Even the bloody dog.'

'Which in a way she did,' said Trythall. 'Her rag had paid over good money. Or promised to. So she acted as if she owned them. That's what cheque-book journalism's about. Then you came muscling in, wanting a share of the action and you hadn't paid a bean. She didn't think that was right; didn't see why you should get something for nothing. So you could say she decided to teach you a lesson. Nothing personal. I'll say that for Deirdre, she didn't get personal. Right bloody nuisance, but always good for a kiss and make-up over a stiff drink in the bar afterwards. No malice in Deirdre.' He stroked his chin thoughtfully, grimaced and said, 'Well, maybe that's a bit of an exaggeration. Perhaps there was a bit of malice in Deirdre. In fact, now I think about it, there's probably a lot of malice in her. But she was always very nice to me. I wouldn't take it personally. She was just doing her job, protecting her territory, and in *Wotcha!* terms it's a good story.'

Their drinks arrived, followed shortly afterwards by their first courses. The Poona Prawn was exactly like the prawn cocktail Trythall had been eating at the Imperial for more than twenty years, completely unaffected by the restaurant's turbanization. The samosas, though a new venture, had obviously been brought in from some mass-production unit in Southall or Bradford. Nothing wrong with them, just mass-produced. Tudor found himself wondering if Thomas Hardy had ever eaten at the Imperial, Sandbourne. Bound to have done, he decided, though he wouldn't have had samosas. Nor even prawn cocktail.

'Sorry,' he said aware that Eddie was talking but not having heard what he had to say. I was thinking about something else. Someone else.'

'Don't tell me,' said Trythall, 'bloody Thomas Hardy. Tell you what, he'd have been a bloody vegetarian. I wish you'd get him out of your system. He's a novelist. Dead novelist. Not relevant. Waste of space.'

He crammed some pink-stained shredded lettuce into his mouth angrily.

'Tell me more about La Robinson,' said

231

Tudor, not wanting to get into a literary argument with his old friend, still thinking the great novelist was relevant in some peculiar way that he couldn't yet explain.

Trythall wasn't stupid. He knew what Cornwall was doing. He didn't particularly like it, but for all sorts of reasons, he was prepared to go along with it.

'She's driven,' he said, 'always has been. We first came up against her when she was with Green Gnome.'

'Green Gnome?'

Eddie Trythall pushed his glass of strawberry-and-cream-coloured rabbit food away from him and took a swig of Tally-ho!

'Green Gnome . . . Red Dwarf . . . Black Midget . . . Vertically challenged Brown-job . . . Blue Person of Restricted Growth . . . I've forgotten. I'm sure it was a primary-coloured diminutive. Beyond that . . .' He shrugged. 'I'm pretty sure it was green because she was the ultimate eco-warrior, going into battle with open-toed sandals and an organic beetroot sandwich. You know the sort of thing. Bloody terrifying. Specially to us poor bloody carnivores.'

'How come she's ended up as a hackette on the ultimate blokes' magazine?'

Trythall shrugged as the Latvian Sikh removed their dishes. 'Dunno,' he said. 'I guess *Wotcha!* recruits from all over the place.'

'Seems a funny sort of choice,' said Tudor,

'both for her and for them.'

'Died-in-the-wool lefties are always turning into different sort of cranks,' said Eddie, with what sounded like feeling. 'The point about Deirdre was that she was extreme. One of the great haters. Everything black and white. Writing for a magazine like *Wotcha!* is a good way of making life horrible for your victims. She'd enjoy that. And she liked being odd. A natural outsider. I admired her in a funny sort of way.'

'I can see that,' said Tudor.

Their main courses arrived. The curry looked conventional and even appetizing. The Curzon dish looked much like any other steak and kidney pudding except for a dollop of mango chutney on the side, a curious gastronomic genuflection to the taste of the Raj.

'Her mobile number is in there,' said Eddie. 'Thought you might like to give her a bell. After all, she owes you one.'

He had lowered his voice to a conspiratorial whisper though none of the other tables was close enough for eavesdropping and the charabanc-load of pensioners and the brace of probable bank managers did not appear to have the potential of eavesdroppers.

'Why would I want to talk to the woman? I'd rather she heard from my solicitors.'

Trythall shovelled a slab of suet into his mouth and shook his head.

'That would be exceedingly foolish. Nobody who means anything will have read the piece in *Wotcha!* Nobody else is going to pick it up. Ignore it and it will go away. Sue and you'll be all over every newspaper and radio station in Britain. TV too. And not in the way you want. Forget it. Turn the other cheek. The one thing Deirdre won't be expecting from you is a friendly call. If I know my girl her response will be to tell you what you want to know.'

'Which is?' It was a rhetorical question but Tudor still wanted Eddie's answer.

'Who really killed Al or Alec, or whoever he was. And whether there is the slightest trace of anything at all in your Thomas Hardy academic garbage.'

Tudor chewed on his perfectly acceptable chicken curry and wondered whether to go down the banana and coconut route. He decided against.

'You think Deirdre will know who the murderer was?'

Eddie took a slug of Tally ho! and swirled it round his mouth ruminatively before wiping froth from his moustache and saying, 'Deirdre got an unexpected bonus story out of you. The next one, the one she's paid for, is about sleaze in an ancient bus, a vicar's son with an under-age girl, petty crime, prostitution. It's all good *Wotcha!* stuff and, frankly, it's all good *Wotcha!* stuff whether our friend in Wintoncester gaol is innocent or not. To be honest, the argument about whether or not she dunnit is a bit abstruse for your average *Wotcha!* reader. As a matter of fact, a guilty verdict will suit Deirdre better than anything else. Having said that, however, she'll have found out from the two of them whodunit. She may not reveal the truth, not if it doesn't suit the story. But she'll know the truth and if you play your cards right she might tell you what it is.'

'Don't see why,' said Tudor.

'You don't know Deirdre,' said Eddie. 'Take it from me, if you eat humble pie, she'll tell.'

'And you? What do you think?' Guilty or not guilty?'

Trythall sighed.

'Would you believe me if I said I don't care very much?'

Tudor looked at his old friend with sympathy but disapproval.

'I think I might believe you, but I'd be sad all the same. I've always thought of you as a policeman who believed in the truth and in justice.'

Eddie pushed more pudding on to his fork.

'I thought of myself like that too,' he said. 'Maybe still do. But look, in this case the girl says she did it and there are no other serious suspects.'

'Well . . .' Tudor demurred.

Eddie's mouth was full so there was a pause while he chewed and swallowed.

'I said *serious.* Your Angel may have done

him in but you'd have a hell of a job proving it, especially when you've got the girl protesting her guilt at the same time.'

'All right,' said Tudor, 'I'll put it another way. Do you think the girl did kill him?'

This time Eddie needed surprisingly little time to think.

'No,' he said, 'as a matter of fact, I don't.'

'Why not?'

This time the policeman did take time to consider. Eventually he said, 'Gut feeling, I suppose. When you've been around crime and criminals as long as I have I think you're entitled. You develop a sixth sense. Wouldn't stand up in court. Lawyers hate it. Jurors much the same. It's like Ulster in the worst days. The army knew perfectly well who the bad guys were. On both sides. But their hands were tied. They were going out on patrol and there were murderers from both sides—Catholics and Proddies—openly laughing at them. Same with us. You *know* who the villains and the bad buggers are but they keep on getting off. Makes you cynical after a while. So I'm not sure you can blame me if I don't weep tears when someone's convicted of something they didn't do. In this case she's bad news anyway. If she didn't kill him, she could have, so why not bang her up before she does kill?'

Tudor wasn't sure he had an answer to this.

They finished their main courses in silence. Then Trythall ordered a marmalade sponge while Tudor opted for a fresh fruit salad.

'Doesn't matter whether she did or she didn't, she'll still go down,' said Cornwall, not sure whether this was a statement or a question. 'And,' he added, 'you don't care one way or the other.' The same applied to this second sentence. Could have been a question. Might have been a statement.

'Nope,' said Trythall, 'I'm not particularly proud of it. But, no, I don't care. Might have done, once. Might again in the future. But not right now. It may be wrong but it's life. Not fair. Not just. Not right. But that's it. That's life.'

Their puddings arrived. The fruit salad looked as sad and limp as Tudor felt. The marmalade pudding matched Trythall's stodgy despondency.

'Where do you think Deirdre stands on this?' asked the reader in Criminal Studies.

'Deirdre just wants a good story. I don't suppose she gives a flying fuck about the truth. Not any more.'

'And the Hardy connection?'

Eddie Trythall laughed mirthlessly.

'She may write comics but that doesn't mean she reads books,' he said. He paused briefly. 'You reckon Arsenal have any chance at Old Trafford on Saturday?' he asked.

CHAPTER TWENTY-FIVE

Tudor's flat in Market Mansions was a classic bachelor pad. It was not uncomfortable. The queen size bed was adequately sprung and mattressed; the sofa and chairs in the drawing-room would not have disgraced a respectable gentlemen's club; the dining area had a pine table with six chairs from Habitat; the kitchen was clean—thanks to the twice weekly visit of Mrs Barnes—and the gas stove had hob and working oven. The wine rack was three-quarters full of decent stuff and the cut-glass whisky decanter was full of Famous Grouse. The study walls were hung with school and university photographs and several of his parents and other relations, now all dead. Elsewhere Cornwall's collection of local land- and sea-scapes alleviated the stark white of his walls. They were good of their kind, but they were not exactly soft or friendly. The estate agents would have described the flat as a 'penthouse apartment' for it was on the top floor. Sliding glass doors gave out on to a balcony with views of Casterbridge and pots of lavender and rosemary, regularly watered by Mrs Barnes.

What it lacked was the feminine touch. This judgement was a touch unfair on Mrs Barnes who was a conscientious cleaner, duster and scrubber—in a literal sense. But even if she had had the nerve to soften Dr Cornwall's austere tastes she also, in a peculiarly Wessex manner, lacked the feminine touch.

Tudor recognized the deficiency and deplored it. He knew far better than anyone else that there was an emptiness in his soul and that this was reflected in his home. He accepted the place but it was not a nest or a haven and he could not love it.

Still, it was where he slept, where he retreated, where, heaven help him, in the last analysis, he lived.

The evening after his Viceregal lunch with Eddie Trythall he had essays to mark, so promised himself a quiet night. He would watch Channel Four News followed by 'University Challenge', cook an omelette, pour a glass of wine, listen to a Mozart opera on disk (there being nothing worth watching between the early Paxman show and the later 'Newsnight'.) The evening would pass pleasantly enough, despite the exasperation he anticipated when reading some of his pupils' essays.

Nevertheless there was emptiness within. He knew that other people would urge him to 'Get a life'! He was comfortable with his own company, self-reliant, contained and content, on the whole and up to a point, to spend time alone with himself. Yet he found himself thinking wistfully about love and friendship and other people. He thought of Ashley Carpenter whom he had considered his best friend at university, whom he had thought of as a friend for life until he discovered his mistake. He thought of little Elizabeth Burney with whom he supposed he was at least half in love but whom, he knew perfectly well, was out of bounds on any number of counts. He thought of Eddie Trythall and wondered if he were a friend or an acquaintance. He thought of his parents and wished he had known them better, taken more trouble, loved them more. He thought of his colleagues, he thought of his pupils.

He thought of thinking about the past but discarded the idea. It was too painful. He regretted having no children now that it was, realistically and in all fairness, too late. He regretted having no wife nor mistress. He regretted the lost opportunities, the failure to commit, the lack of serious risk-taking, the over-concentration on work and career, the inability to have fun, to relax, to let hair down. He was sorry that other people increasingly regarded him as a dry stick; sorrier still that, increasingly, they had a point. He had a capacity for affection, for unselfishness, for whatever it was that made humans human; but he felt that quality draining away from him, almost by the minute.

He poured himself a stiff Famous Grouse and reflected that it was several months since

240

he had poured another person a Scotch from his own decanter. He could barely remember when anyone other than Mrs Barnes had crossed the door-mat, let alone when he had actually entertained. Perhaps he should stage a drinks party, or a dinner. Who would he invite? The Trythalls? Little Miss Burney? A pupil or two? Colleagues? Perhaps he should advertise in one of the more respectable 'Men seeking women' columns. The *Oldie* perhaps. 'Fifty-something academic; GSOH; non-smoker; exotic motor car; southern England; seeks similar for friendship possibly more'. He winced, shuddered and told himself to stop succumbing to self-pity. He was successful; on the verge of modest fame; fit, healthy; reasonable looking; solvent; but lonely and emotionally-unfulfilled.

'Oh shut up,' he said out loud. Maybe he should buy a dog. He thought fondly of Basil, the Ozzie mutt he had befriended in Tasmania. Perhaps a Basil would cheer him up. But even the thought was an admission of defeat.

He supposed he should phone the Deirdre woman. Immersion in the D'Urberville murders was one way of taking himself out of himself, of forgetting his problems. God knows they weren't problems compared with the main actors in those sad cases—the corpses, the condemned, the down, the out. How dare he feel sorry for himself when there were other

241

people who really were up against it. Even so he did not want to phone Deirdre Robinson. He drank some Grouse and decided to put her off until after supper and TV. Cowardice possibly, but a little Dutch courage would not come amiss.

He read a couple of essays. One by Freddie and one by Karl. Freddie's was beta with possibly a touch of alpha; Karl's was disappointing. He marked Freddie b?a and gave Karl a b- with comments to match. He was bored by beta. Only Elizabeth Burney struck him as having consistent alpha qualities but he acknowledged that there was personal bias involved in this assessment.

He put the papers down. Turned on the TV in the kitchen, cracked open three eggs, whipped them up with a fork, seasoned them; melted some butter in a frying pan and wondered whether or not to slice a tomato as a side-salad. He decided against and opened a bottle of Montepulciano instead.

It was a slack news day. Even the silkily garrulous Jon Snow in his usual fluorescent necktie seemed to be struggling. Tudor was always struck by the constraints of programming as with those of editing in the print media. It didn't make sense to Tudor to devote the same amount of time or space to news every day no matter what. It was perfectly obvious that some days were dull and some interesting, yet television had, in a sense, to treat them all as if they were exactly the same.

Today, he felt, munching through a perfectly edible but essentially boring omelette, was a dull day. During 'University Challenge' he ate a couple of apricots. He liked apricots and believed they were good for him. Paxman was his usual ebullient self, chivying two teams of rather nondescript students from institutions of which Tudor had not previously heard. The University of Wessex had entered a team the previous year, ignoring the claims of his students from Criminal Studies. They had been knocked out in the first round by one of the dimmer Oxford colleges. Tudor had been quietly satisfied but, wisely, kept his sentiments to himself.

Challenge over, Tudor snapped off the TV, debated whether to listen to *Figaro* or *Don Giovanni* and opted for the latter. After the overture and an aria or two he remembered the dreaded Deirdre. For a moment he thought seriously about postponing the call until the following day. Much better listen to Mozart, he thought, but then realized he was being feeble.

'Man's gotta do what a man's gotta do,' he said, out loud, turning down the music and picking up the Deirdre file that Eddie Trythall had given him over lunch. She sounded a prize bitch in both incarnations. He didn't want to talk to her but he knew that he would never forgive himself if he didn't. Nor would Eddie, which, in a way, was even worse. And, who knows, the ghastly woman might just have the key to the problem which was obsessing him.

He couldn't be bothered with Deirdre's early career and her various confrontations with the police in Sandbourne. She sounded, to Tudor, like the standard-issue, know-all, bolshie, revolutionary green-goddess. Not his type.

He picked up his mobile with a sigh of anticipatory disgust. And pressed the relevant buttons. There were enough unanswered rings to make him anticipate an automatic nobody-here response and he was on the verge of a relieved hang-up when a metallic, nasal voice answered.

'Yes,' it said, in a deliberately uncommunicative way.

'Deirdre Robinson?' said Tudor.

'This is she,' said the Dalek voice.

'Good evening,' said Tudor, 'it's Tudor Cornwall, University of Wessex. We met the other day in the D'Urberville bus. I read your piece about me in *Wotcha!*'

She didn't hang up. He had half expected her to.

The silence needed to be broken. He broke it.

'I thought it was very interesting.'

Another silence.

'I'm not apologizing.'

Tudor could almost smell years of nicotine coming down the woman's nostrils and across the ether.

'I wouldn't even suggest it,' he said. 'You're entitled to your opinion. Like me. We're both grown-ups. I'm sure we can agree to differ. As it happens I have much the same opinion of journalists as you have of academics but so what?'

'How did you get my number?' she asked.

'Let's just say,' he said, 'that academics don't live in quite the sort of cut-off ivory towers that some people think.'

'*Touché,*' said the woman from *Wotcha!* 'So you don't want an apology. What exactly do you want?'

Tudor looked round the Spartan comforts of his home and found himself asking what exactly he did want. Nothing that Deirdre Robinson could provide. On the other hand she might be able to help with the short-term specifics. And only by coming to terms with the short-term specifics could he begin to grapple with the long-term, all-embracing stuff and sort himself out.

'I need to know who committed murder. I need to know whether the girl killed her man. I need to know whether she's as guilty as she says she is. I need to know what you've paid for.'

Over the phone he heard her strike a light, draw on the illuminated cigarette and exhale down the line.

'I've paid for the story of a way of life and a situation which I believe will interest my readers,' she said, eventually. 'It's not my job to interfere with the course of justice. I leave that to people like you. I don't share your arrogance.'

Tudor bit his lip. He must not lose his temper. That would be counter-productive. Demeaning as well. Bad idea on every count.

'Listen,' he said, 'I don't want to trade insults. As I said I'd prefer to agree to disagree. However I believe there is a grave danger of a serious miscarriage of justice. If the couple whose story you've bought have been as honest as I'd hope then you might be able to shed some helpful light.'

'It's not part of my brief to buy someone's story and then have them convict themselves of murder.'

'I'm not asking that,' said Tudor. 'It's just that I don't believe the girl is guilty. I don't believe she did it. If there is anything you can tell me which would help get her off I'd be hugely grateful.'

'Supposing she doesn't want to get off,' said the voice. 'That's my understanding. I think she wants to be found guilty even if she isn't.'

Tudor recognized truth in this.

'Did anyone talk about Thomas Hardy? The author? *Tess of the D'Urbervilles*? There's something there but I don't know what.'

A laugh came down the line.

'I gave up reading books a long time ago,' she said. 'Hard enough writing words without having to read them.'

Another silence. Tudor thought she was going to hang up on him.

'Since you ask though,' she said, 'we talked about the book you mention. From what I understand there are answers in there but the odds are all against anyone finding them. You included. Thanks for calling. I appreciate it.'

There was a click. The line went dead. He poured himself a stiff Scotch and, Mozart having finished, turned the TV back on again. He didn't really see and he didn't really listen but he thought a lot about the answer in the book.

CHAPTER TWENTY-SIX

South-west fourteen, the London postal district to which Tudor and Elizabeth had been led by the green rings in the dead man's copy of *Tess of the D'Urbervilles* was a salubrious suburb in a leafy pocket of the metropolis unserved by the Underground railway and ill-served by any other form of public transport. Partly because of this and partly because the houses were mostly handsome and huge as well as being garlanded with gardens, the district had taken on an air of relentless bourgeois prosperity. It was, thought Tudor, good burglar country.

They took the overground railway from Waterloo and rattled through Clapham and Putney in an ancient and grubby carriage which would not have seemed modern even in the more deprived countries of Eastern Europe. Tudor increasingly often felt that Britain in general and London in particular were coming apart at the seams. It made his professional life more rewarding, but personally he found the gradual descent into lawlessness distressing.

They passed a Victorian school with children running around in the asphalt playground.

'That's where you learn to be a gangster,' he said to the girl. 'The three Rs of modern life: rape, robbery and racism, frequently running together in an unholy trinity.'

She smiled at him. 'Isn't that unduly cynical?' she asked.

'Put *my* cynicism down to age and *your* optimism to innocence,' he said.

'Unduly cynical,' she said, still laughing at him. 'You're not that old and I'm not that young either. So I can't be that innocent which means my optimism is not misplaced.'

'Bloody Australian,' he said, laughing now.

'Bloody Pom,' she replied, laughing too.

She was wearing tight jeans, clunky knee-high boots, a black leather top and was carrying a designer handbag from Orca. Her blonde hair was thick and lustrous, her complexion fresh and scrubbed. She was bewitching and Tudor suddenly felt old and sad and grey.

They got out at a run-down, unmanned station surrounded by allotments and besmirched by graffiti. In all his life of crime Tudor had never ever seen anyone spraying graffiti or vandalizing such commonplace targets as unmanned railway stations or bus-stops. In view of the high incidence of these activities this was surprising, particularly as he had a professional interest in crime of all sorts, however petty.

He had an A-Z with him and this indicated that the local King's Road lay to the north near the River Thames. The day was clear and crisp though the allotments had a bleak frozen wintry air to them. In one of them, an old man in an army surplus great coat scratched at the unyielding earth with a hoe and Tudor was once again reminded of Eastern Europe. He had seen Bulgarian peasants looking more up-to-date than the solitary pensioner hacking away at his little patch of England. He half expected to see women in black smocks driving donkey carts or to be accosted by children selling individual hen's eggs as he had been once in a subway in St Petersburg.

Beyond the allotments, however, affluence

249

returned with many of its early twenty-first century ramifications—a designer pub called The Shit and Shovel, a fishmonger with squid, scallops and seabass on the slab, estate agents advertising Victorian villas at over a million pounds each, Porsches and Bentleys parked on double yellow lines, a florist with exotic African and Antipodean blooms fresh from Heathrow Airport and a million miles from the infertile allotments behind them. This was Cool Britannia in all its consumer-led, lifestyle glory. It seemed a long way even from Wessex and Digby Matravers let alone a bogstandard B and B in Sandbourne, an old bus in the Stonehenge car-park or a solitary cell in Wintoncester gaol.

They were closing in now, he thought as they came to a crossroads and saw that this glitzy drag named Garibaldi Street was here bisected by the King's Road running east and west. He was reminded momentarily of Angel Clare and Tess's elfin sister Liza-Lu, standing on the hill overlooking the city and waiting for the black flag to be raised and signify that the President of the Immortals had finished his sport with the heroine of the great novel. He was no Angel and Elizabeth no Liza-Lu but, like the duo in the fiction of 1890, they were nearing a conclusion, a resolution of all that had gone before.

They were looking for number 248 and Tudor's A-Z indicated that this lay to the east and on the north side of the road towards the Thames. The houses here were narrow Georgian properties with brass plates offering the services of the professional classes—lawyers, accountants, doctors and dentists, brokers and financial advisers, hearing-aid consultants, undertakers even.

They passed 222 which was a solicitors' office; 236 which was a debt collector—dingier than its neighbours; and then they were on the door-step of 248. Journey's end.

'Do you want to go on?' he asked, 'or do you think you've made a ridiculous mistake? It's not too late to turn back.'

'Why ever should we?' she wanted to know. 'The clues were all there, all the time. You're only sceptical because for once you didn't see them and you're embarrassed. And it's obviously the right place. Just look at the name plate.'

Tudor looked, though he sensed without looking that the girl was right. She nearly always was.

The sign said 'Trudgeon and Trounce, Solicitors and Commissioners of Oaths'. Est. 1890.'

The two of them stood gazing at the words in what might have passed for a respectful silence until Elizabeth said, 'These are they then. We'd better go in. Which do you think: Trudgeon or Trounce?'

It turned out to be Trounce. The last

Trudgeon had passed away shortly after the end of World War Two leaving the business entirely in the hands of the Trounces though that wasn't strictly speaking true since a Trudgeon had married a Trounce some time in the thirties and the present senior partner, Mr Paget Trounce, was a product of this union and could therefore claim to be as much of a Trudgeon as a Trounce. His sons and grandsons were also working for the firm and although outsiders joined from time to time none had ever ascended to a partnership and the present day firm was in effect, Trounce, Trounce, Trounce, Trounce and Trounce.

Paget Trounce Senior, through the medium of a bored and blousy blonde receptionist, asked the visitors to kindly step into his office. Paget Trounce Junior was his in-house grandson, for the Christian name had recurred every second generation for as long as anyone could remember. Paget Trounce Junior, the spitting image of his grandfather, between forty and fifty years younger, sat in but said nothing.

Both men were extraordinarily etiolated, as if they had been incarcerated in the office at 248 King's Road for their entire lives, whitening in the artifical light until they were drained of all colour: They resembled a couple of white rabbits, albino save for their pink-rimmed eyes. Even their dark suits seemed sucked dry by the oak-panelled gloom of their official surroundings.

252

'We've been expecting you, Dr Cornwall,' said Paget Trounce Senior at which Paget Trounce Junior nodded in agreement, lips furled back over yellowing, smoker's teeth.

'Though not,' continued the senior partner, 'your, er, assistant. Our client made no mention of anyone other than yourself.'

'Miss Burney is studying for a doctorate at the University of Wessex under my supervision,' said Tudor. 'And your client?'

'Ah, yes, our client. Our client would have deposited these papers before Miss Burney commenced her doctorate I fancy.' His thin lips, parted and drew back over the gums, just as his grandson's had.

There was a an awkward silence and then Trounce continued, 'Our client stipulated only that if and when you presented yourself here we should hand over the papers that he had marked for your attention. We will of course require proof of identity and a signature by way of receipt. That is all. Our client imposed no further conditions.'

Another pause as pregnant as the first. Tudor would like to have asked something but decided to wait. Trounce Senior evidently used long pauses for punctuation—a Pinter of the legal profession. In a moment or two he cleared his throat phlegmily and resumed.

'I am not required in law,' said the dessicated old man, 'to say anything more than I have already. Nevertheless I feel that by way

253

of clarification and by way of service to the deceased I should say a few words of clarification and perhaps even of mitigation.'

Both Trounces were holding their hands together, the finger-tips meeting under their chins, the gesture halfway between prayer and contemplation. Their similarity, both in appearance and mannerism, was disquieting.

'Our client first came to us when apprehended on a charge of fraudulently passing off luxury motor-cars.'

'Stolen?' interrupted Tudor, who was becoming irritated by the funereal pace of this exposition.

'Oh, not at all.' Paget Trounce Senior allowed himself another of his trademark humourless grins. 'All Al's limousines were honestly acquired.'

'Alec?' Tudor enquired. He was more interested in nomenclature than second-hand cars.

'Al, Albert, Alec, Alex, Alexander, Alan, Alvin, Algernon . . . His Christian names always began Al but I never knew quite which he was using from one day to the next, so I compromised by always thinking of him as Al. But in a manner of speaking I don't think he had what you'd call a "real" name any more than he had what you'd call a "real" identity. He was a number of different people masquerading as the same. Quite the reverse of what others thought. His enemies tended to assume he was one person pretending to be a whole lot of others, but Al wasn't like that. He had a multiple personality. Never the same person really. More like a squadron of almost identical twins. He was the most stimulating client and, as I said, the limousines were honestly acquired. He rather disapproved of stealing vehicles.'

'So, if they weren't stolen what was the nature of the crime?' asked Tudor.

'Ah.' Mr Trounce shut his eyes momentarily and bared his teeth in yet another wintry grin. 'He was tinkering with the mileage clocks, but his most engaging er, "scam" I think would be the *mot juste*, related to previous ownerships. I could never really bring myself to think of it as a crime in the accepted sense. He was simply telling a tall story and taking advantage of his clients' innate snobbery. Rather admirable. And, I'm happy to say, that on most occasions we were able to persuade juries to take a similar point of view.'

'Telling tall stories about Rolls Royces,' said Elizabeth. 'Could you elaborate? I'm not sure I'm with you.'

'Most people who buy expensive automobiles,' said Mr Trounce, in the patronizing manner of a headmaster addressing the new intake, 'do so for social rather than motoring reasons. Al took advantage of the fact and when selling one of his Rolls Royces would inform the purchaser, out of the side of his mouth as it were, that the vehicle in question, although the log book was too discreet to reveal such a matter, once been in the ownership of, shall we say, Sir Bernard and Lady Docker, Sir Gerald Nabarro, the Maharajah of Baroda or even a minor member of the House of Windsor. The price of the car would then escalate accordingly. You'd be surprised to know how much extra a certain sort of *arriviste* will pay for a limousine that once belonged to the Duke of Windsor . . . or even Sir Gerald Nabarro.'

'Was passing Rollers off as the former property of posh people his only crime?' asked Tudor not altogether innocently.

Mr Trounce Senior looked arch. 'Good heavens no,' he said. 'The celebrity car conceit was just one of his cunning wheezes. He had a number of credit-card wheezes. There was a deplorable escapade when he contrived to induce a number of perfectly respectable women to have intercourse with him on the grounds that he was an official inspector researching on behalf of the National Statistical Survey into Sexually Transmitted Diseases. We were unable to prevent a custodial sentence in that case, I fear. In fact sex got him into more trouble than anything else. When times were really hard he put his poor wife to work. There was a wretched business with a massage parlour in Peckham. He was a useful forger and counterfeiter when the need arose. And, naturally, a master of disguise. On at least one occasion I completely failed to recognize him.'

Mr Trounce sighed. 'I often wonder,' he said, 'what would have happened to him had he had the benefit of further education. He was, in many respects, a remarkable personality and a formidable intellect!'

Silence fell on the panelled room like a final curtain.

At last Mr Trounce took off his glasses, polished them briefly with a pocket handkerchief, put them back on again, coughed and picked up an envelope which had been lying on the desk.

'This,' he said, handing it to Tudor, 'is the letter he wrote for you. I haven't read it.'

Cornwall took the long buff envelope. On it in a loopy backward-slanting hand were the words 'Dr Tudor Cornwall. To await arrival.'

'Supposing I hadn't come?' he said.

'We discussed that,' said the lawyer. 'I pointed out that we knew your place of abode and could send it to you by registered post. But he was most adamant that you had to come here. He said he had set a little puzzle. He didn't appear to think you would have difficulty in solving it but he was most adamant that we were not to put it in the post. I remember his words quite distinctly. He said, "I'm not going to make it easy for the . . ." Well, let's just say that the epithet he applied was not intended to flatter.'

He adjusted his glasses once more, cleared his throat.

'And this,' he said, picking up a bulky folder tied, like a brief, with vivid pink ribbon, 'is also for you. The deceased said something about it being his posthumous doctoral thesis—a remark I'm afraid I was unable to fathom but which I can only assume was a not wholly untypical piece of whimsy or flight of fancy.'

He smiled a thin smile and handed the folder across the desk.

'And so Dr Cornwall,' he said, rising, 'I'll bid you good day. Should there be anything in these papers that you wish to discuss you know where to find me. He left everything else to Mrs D'Urberville, though as you can probably guess there was precious little to leave.'

'I'll bet,' said Tudor.

He and Elizabeth rose to go and were shown out by the silent grandson.

Outside in the street three old scarlet Routemaster double decker buses rumbled past in tight formation.

'Let's find somewhere a bit friendlier and see what the old fraud wants to tell us,' he said.

Elizabeth nodded and they both shivered, though not from the cold.

CHAPTER TWENTY-SEVEN

There was a Starbuck's at the end of the street next to a curious Albanian restaurant called Enver's which looked as if it were a front for something nefarious.

Elizabeth ordered a cappuccino and Tudor a double espresso.

'Read it to me,' she said, as he opened the envelope and quickly scanned the enclosed sheets of lined handwritten pages.

He shrugged, sipped and did as he was told.

'Dear Doctor Cornwall,' he began. *'You've obviously solved my little puzzle or you wouldn't be reading this. If I'm right and you couldn't wait to open this surprise packet then you'll have gone to Starbuck's if it's outside eating hours or to Enver's if you're having lunch. I wouldn't recommend Enver's: named after Mr Hoxha, the late and unlamented President of Albania. They do kebabs made from meat that fell off the back of a lorry, salads of soggy tomatoes and under-cooked rice. There's a half-decent orange liqueur and the girls are pretty and will give you a bloody good time for not much cash-in-hand.*

'But, as you literary types would say, I digress. Oh dope too, if you're into that sort of thing. But they are *Albanian Mafiosi. Nice blokes but they cut corners so you might have a bad trip.*

Anyway, wherever you are I'm glad we've finally made contact even though by the time you read this I'll be dead and you, presumably, will still be alive. "Such is life," as Ned Kelly said on the scaffold. Now there, if you don't mind me wandering off again, is an interesting criminal. Have you read Peter Carey's novel? Not bad, especially for an Australian.'

'Excuse me,' said Elizabeth, 'that's a bit gratuitous. Ozlit is extremely fashionable, as you know.'

'You should know about British prejudices regarding your fellow countrymen,' said Tudor. 'And you're just as bad. All those jokes about soap. But that's not the point, is it? Al or Albert or Alec or whoever he was doesn't sound like a small-time professional criminal, he sounds, well—'

'Quite bright,' said the girl, 'and literate. Reads Booker prize-winners for Chris'sake.'

'There's no law that says minor crooks have to be stupid.'

'No but . . .' she protested.

'May I continue?' he asked.

'Of course.'

Tudor coughed, uneasily aware that it sounded a bit like an echo of Paget Trounce Senior's expectoration.

'I dare say you'd like me to begin at the beginning,' he read, *'but as you and I know only*

260

too well the classic crime story starts at the end. A murder mystery is as dependent on a corpse as habeas corpus. Without a body you don't have a book; without a murder there's no story. So beginning at the beginning is the wrong approach in a situation such as this. On the other hand, you already have your stiff. That's me. I wonder if I've been disposed of yet? I asked for a cremation job which I guess I'll get. On the other hand if Tess is binned up and on a murder rap and if the Angel of Clare is as flaky as I've always supposed, then who knows? I suppose I wouldn't mind if most of my mortal remains were used for medical research but it's not what I asked for. Oh well. I'll know sod all about it and by the time you read this I'll either be in a far, far better place or nowhere at all. But, as I say, you have your mortality so perhaps I may be allowed to back-track at once.

'This is a bit like I imagine writing an obituary must be. You have your set-up first paragraph or so, then you clear your throat and say that the deceased was born on such and such a day in such and such a month of such and such a year. And then you plod through the life like we used to do English history at Osmington with one thing always leading to another which, in my experience, isn't true because my life has always been a journey of dead-ends, cul-de-sacs and unexpected obstacles and obstructions. Particularly now. Writing this I know that I will be dead in approximately twenty-four hours' time

261

because. But I'm getting ahead of myself. Too much digression and sidestep. One of the many problems in my life so far. Well, my life, full stop or bloody nearly. I wonder sometimes if you had been more, well, whatever all those years ago but then, we'll never know now will we? Water under the bridge, blood spilt to no purpose or whatever.

'Never knew my dad. Never liked my mum. Those aren't excuses. Happens to thousands of us and lots turn out normal. Nice even. Not that I think of myself as abnormal or un-nice. One doesn't, does one? I mean I think you're a complete shit but I don't suppose you feel the same. Why should you? You've endless reasons for inflated self-esteem. But I mustn't go on. This is about me not about you. Well, except that in a manner of speaking it's about the two of us, isn't it?'

'What's he on about?' asked Elizabeth, wiping cappuccino froth from her upper lip, 'I'm getting confused. You and he seem to have a shared past. What's that about? Did you know him? I thought he was a complete stranger'.

'So did I,' said Tudor thoughtfully, 'but evidently that's not a view he shared.'

He rubbed his jaw ruefully, sipped at his strong black coffee and went back to reading out loud.

'I was an only child in a single-parent family

262

which I guess is never a bundle of laughs. Ordinary state primary school. Very little money. Few friends. I'm not trying to make you feel sorry for me, just stating facts. Don't know when I started reading books but I was very young. It was the best way I could find to escape what people call "reality". And I took to crime when I was small as well. Not that I thought of it as crime when I began. More like a way of redressing an unfairness. Robin Hood stuff Except that I never gave anyone else anything that I nicked. Kept it for myself And why not? It's what the rich people did.

'So fast forward. I won a place at Osmington. All right it was a crap school but it was better than anything I'd known before and they had a fantastic English teacher. God knows what he was doing there. He was gay, of course, but I never heard that stopped people being employed at schools like Eton and Winchester and he was easily good enough for a school like that. He was the biz. Really. And he took a shine to me. It wasn't just the sex. I think he was genuinely fond of me and he taught me about English literature and words and things like what tintinnabulation meant and onomatopoeia and assonance and what an iambic pentameter was and a dactyl and a trochee—all that shit that nobody bothers with these days.

And then I had to leave. I still don't know what it was all about. A bit of sex, a bit of stealing, a bit of money problems back home.

Don't ask me. One day I was there and the next I wasn't. Nobody explained properly. It was all wrapped up in, well, to be honest, I don't know what it was wrapped up in but by then I'd discovered Hardy and the Wessex countryside and especially Tess.

'Tess *was my bible. Still is. All that inevitability bit, the having no control, being pushed around by the President of the sodding Immortals whoever they might be. They sound like a rock band. But it started me thinking about all this crime stuff, about good and bad, and right and wrong, and which side of the law you end up on, and getting banged up for things that weren't your fault. Seemed to me that maybe you didn't have any choice. It was all decided before you were born. And what was decided for me was being what the rest of you buggers call a crook, a villain, a criminal, whatever. Don't get me wrong. I don't believe in violence or cruelty or any of that. But we'll get to that a bit later because of course by the time you read this I'll have died a violent death which maybe goes against my whole philosophy. But then again maybe not.'*

'He's barking,' said Elizabeth.

'But barking in an intriguing way. He's beginning to sound like a case history. Worth a paper wouldn't you say? Essay in learned journal? "Crime and the premature school leaver"? "Fantasy and Felony". What do

264

you think?'

'I think you should read on.'

'Oh, OK. Unputdownable.'

'Well,' she said, 'at least I want to know what happened next.'

'*Sorry,*' read Tudor, '*I'm not going to give you my entire life story. You'll get most of it from Tess and the Angel anyway. Tell you what, if you want a less partial source, you could do worse than have a word with the Vicar of Digby Matravers. Funny old boy. The Reverend Peter Lillywhite. Horrible wife but he and I always got on. We shared an interest in crime although being a man of the cloth he'd never really tried his hand at it.*

'*Anyway I'll fast forward a bit to the application. You don't remember the application, do you? Maybe you never even saw it. It was just after the Department of Criminal Studies was first set up fifteen years ago. I read a piece about it and about you in the* Telegraph. You *were quoted as mouthing a whole lot of crap about how ground-breaking and revolutionary you were going to be and how you wanted to attract students from all sorts of backgrounds even including the criminal fraternity. So naturally I thought with my back-ground I was a shoe-in. Having done time, committed a number of different so-called or alleged crimes I'd be just the sort of person you'd want on your first foundation course. So I send in a written application complete with CV and I sit and I wait for six weeks and three days and then I get a flat little rejection. It's signed by you but on close inspection it's either a cleverer than usual rubber stamp job or your secretary or whatever has faked it on your behalf Or maybe you did actually sign it yourself without bothering to read the letter much less the application. I was told my application couldn't be considered because I didn't have three "A" levels. As I had more than three convictions and knew several of Her Majesty's prisons from the inside I thought I'd got better qualifications than some snotty kid with three "A" levels. And the interview with you made me think you'd agree. Never believe anything you read in the newspapers.'*

Tudor stopped reading. 'Bugger,' he said. 'I need another coffee.'

Elizabeth said she could use another cappuccino so he went to the counter and returned a minute or so later with two coffees and a grimace.

'We were inundated with applications,' he said. 'We turned away hundreds of perfectly well-qualified applicants.'

'But you should have accepted this one.'

Tudor ran a hand through his hair and sighed.

'Probably.'

'Definitely.'

He smiled feebly. 'If you say so. Though the lack of academic qualifications would have been a problem.'

'Balls,' she said. 'You screwed up. He was

right to feel aggrieved.'

'If you say so. But we were chronically over-worked and under-staffed.'

'That's no excuse.'

'I know, but it's too late to do anything about it. The man's dead.'

'Precisely.'

He looked at her incredulously. 'Are you saying I was in some way to blame for his death?'

'Who knows?' She shrugged. 'We won't know till we've finished the letter, will we?'

'I suppose not.' He picked up the sheets of paper and resumed where he had left off.

'Never believe anything you read in the newspapers,' he repeated. *'It was a disappointment. Of course it was. I really thought I might be good at whatever it is you do. With the utmost respect, as Queen's Counsel are fond of saying—and believe you me I've heard them—with the utmost respect it's all very well dealing in academic theories and the like but until you know what it's actually like to be arrested, and banged up, and cross-examined and sentenced and the whole bit, you don't know what it's like. I don't blame you but you can only imagine what it's like when there's a bang on the front door around dawn and it's Inspector Knacker of the Yard with some of his mates. It's the trouble with all academic stuff. Doesn't matter how clever you are and how well read, you can't understand it unless you've actually*

lived life at the sharp end.

'The clever men at Oxford
Know all that there is to be knowed,
But they none of them know one half as
  much
As intelligent Mr Toad.'

'Well, the University of Wessex isn't exactly Oxford and maybe I'm not exactly Mr Toad but I'm sure you know what I mean and I dare say, deep down, you agree with what I'm saying.

'I'm not a particularly vindictive man but I confess I did want to get my own back. Like I said Tess *has been my bible. Read it all the time. Can recite big chunks of it. But there's a lot that's not right about it. Like I don't think Hardy properly understands Alec. He thinks Alec's a little shit but Alec is as manipulated as everyone else. It's not just the President of the Immortals who's screwing him around it's Tess. It's Hardy. It's the whole world.*

'Tess. My Tess thinks I'm fixated on the book. Obsessed with it. Maybe I am but like I say it's a sort of bible. I guess I kind of live by it which may sound dumb but it's not dumb to say you live by the Bible or the Koran. I've sort of lived by it and by the time you read this I'll have died by it as well. In a manner of speaking, at least, I have theories about the book too. In fact you'll find out all about them in a short while.

'I've always been a smoker. Expensive habit.

268

Not much smoking in Hardy. One or two clay pipes perhaps but I don't remember Sergeant Troy or Michael Henchard having a fag. Could be wrong. It's not only expensive, it's dangerous. I knew that but I sort of like didn't care. Didn't like the way it made me cough and it started to get so that I was having trouble with stairs and stuff. Then I started coughing up blood and the old girl made me see the doctor. And he took one look and sent me off for X-Rays and before I can say more than a word he has me in and tells me I've got the big "C" and I'm lucky if I'll manage another six months.

'So I think well I don't want to die in bloody agony coughing my guts out in some frigging public ward surrounded by a lot of senile pensioners and morphined up to my eyeballs. So I check into a B and B which is pretty much like the one in the book and this is where it gets to be fun . . . I've written the letter to you and given it to old Trounce together with the thesis that you'll see when you've finished this. Then I've gone back to the B and B, staged a flaming row with my girl and, when she walks out, I stab myself with the bread knife.

'My hunch is that like in the book she'll plead guilty to murder because she's had enough, right? She doesn't fancy hanging around with the Angel and she doesn't want to go back on the game so she's better off having a nice spell in the nick. Won't get topped like in the book and three meals a day, central heating and female

269

company, if you know what I mean. But even if she pleads "not guilty" who's going to believe her? Eh? Any case, even if you were to produce this letter in court it's only a statement of intent. You can't prove that I've done what I've said I'll do. I'll be found with a knife in my belly and blood seeping through the carpet just like in the book and I hope to God it's that old bag of a landlady who finds me because she's a dragon and the shock'll do her good.

'So there you have it. I'd better stop now, catch the train, give this to old man Trounce. Don't want to risk the post. Toodlepip. Nice not knowing you. Do what you like with the thesis. A PhD. (Posthumous) would be pukka. You could put it on my headstone. Happy reading and not very best wishes from the best pupil you never had.'

Tudor put down the letter and sipped coffee.

'Barking,' said the girl.

'I don't know,' said Tudor. 'There's a certain sort of warped logic to it all. And I'm sorry we turned him down. Sounds as if he was a lot more stimulating than the average first-year student.'

He turned his attention to the bulky package that came as a codicil to the letter. When he opened the folder it looked as if the contents consisted of a full-length manuscript, handwritten in what was now familiar writing,

270

on one side of the paper, examination style.

Tudor scanned the opening page and then read it out loud.

'*Bed, Blood and Breakfast,*' he intoned. '*A PhD Thesis by Al Smith of no fixed abode and now deceased, based on a novel by Thomas Hardy.*' He turned the page and went very pale.

'*Chapter One,*' he read in a disbelieving strangulated voice, and then after a pause he looked hard at Elizabeth and said, 'You'll never guess how he begins.'

She smiled. 'I think perhaps I might,' she said.

'Go on then,' he said.

She smiled again,

'Drip, drip, drip,' she said.

And when he nodded in confirmation that she was correct she smiled a third time.

'Elementary,' she said.